Praise for Roxy

'A novel you devour in one sitting: elegiac, beautiful, and very strong.'
HERMAN KOCH, author of *The Dinner*

'*Roxy* is a novel to read slowly—like a good wine is to be savored rather than drank down in one gulp.'
Het Parool

'Some sentences in *Roxy* are as if carved in stone; like Samuel Beckett, Gerritsen knows how to capture moments of terrifying precision and darkness.'
De Morgen

'In her fifth book Esther Gerritsen has continued to grow to the level of an author who dares to incorporate every-thing—from comical cross-talk to heartrending silence. Once again, she displays her gift for striking sentences and dialogue that teeters on the thin line between normality and alienation, between entertaining kookiness and harrowing absurdism.'
De Volkskrant

'An excellent new novel from Gerritsen written with inde-structible good cheer.'
NRC Handelsblad

'Even more than we have grown used to, in *Roxy* Gerritsen strips her scenes and language to the bone, leaving us with the core, which is ridiculously good.'
OPZIJ LITERATURE PRIZE

'The stories of Esther Gerritsen, one of the best Dutch writers for years, are always extreme, dramatic, and confrontational. What is so special about Gerritsen's work is that within a somewhat outrageous story she wraps a deeper, existential message.'
Trouw

'Not only in her choice of subjects but also in her feeling for style, Gerritsen is one of a kind. Her absurdist logic and subtle humoristic voice make every sentence in her novels and columns a "typical Gerritsen."'
JURY, FRANS KELLENDONK PRIZE

'Esther Gerritsen's characters have their own, extremely unique way of viewing the world.'
Vogue

Praise for Craving

'The lives of others, in all their peculiarity, are given sympathetic scrutiny in this diverting European oddity, in cool prose and naturalistic dialogue.'
Kirkus Reviews

'I don't know if I've ever read a novel that captures the emotional labor of people-pleasing language quite so well … Droll and horrific and incredibly moving.'
New York Times

'Cool, sparse, and delicious, Esther Gerritsen's *Craving* hits all the right notes. This is an author who is unafraid of both complex characters and complex emotion (Thank God!).'
ALICE SEBOLD, author of *The Lovely Bones*

ESTHER GERRITSEN is a Dutch novelist, columnist, and playwright. She made her literary debut in 2000. She is one of the most widely read and highly praised authors in the Netherlands, and makes regular appearances on radio programs and at international literary festivals, such as Litquake and Wordfest. Esther Gerritsen had the honor of writing the Dutch Book Week gift in 2016, which had a print run of 700,000 copies. In 2014 she was awarded the Frans Kellendonk Prize for her entire oeuvre. Her novel *Craving* was shortlisted for the Vondel Prize and was published in the US in September 2018. *Roxy* has sold over 20,000 copies in the Netherlands and was shortlisted for the Libris Literature Prize.

MICHELE HUTCHISON studied at UEA, Cambridge, and Lyon universities and worked in publishing for a number of years. In 2004, she moved to Amsterdam. Among the many works she has translated are *La Superba* by Ilja Leonard Pfeijffer, *Fortunate Slaves* by Tom Lanoye, *Craving* by Esther Gerritsen, and *An American Princess* by Annejet van der Zijl. She also co-authored the successful parenting book, *The Happiest Kids in the World*.

ROXY

ESTHER GERRITSEN

ROXY

Translated from the Dutch
by Michele Hutchison

WORLD EDITIONS
New York, London, Amsterdam

Published in the USA in 2019 by World Editions LLC, New York
Published in the UK in 2016 by World Editions Ltd., London

World Editions
New York/London/Amsterdam

Printed by Sheridan, Chelsea, MI, USA

Library of Congress Cataloging in Publication Data is available

ISBN 978-1-64286-040-5

First published as *Roxy* in the Netherlands in 2014 by De Geus

The publisher gratefully acknowledges the support of the Dutch
Foundation for Literature

N ederlands
letterenfonds
dutch foundation
for literature

Twitter: @WorldEdBooks
Facebook: WorldEditionsInternationalPublishing
www.worldeditions.org
Book Club Discussion Guides are available on our website.

Dost thou behold
How I, stout heart and bold,
I, the undaunted once in open battle,
Lay violent hands on unsuspecting cattle?
Alas for scorn! How am I put to shame!

Sophocles, *Ajax, translation by Sir George Young*

THERE ARE TWO of them: a man and a woman. The man asks her if she is Roxy—a strange policeman saying her name in the middle of the night. Yes, she is. Can they come in? Roxy would rather they didn't.

She assumes the worst: her husband could be dead. He's always worrying about having a heart attack. He has the risk factors. This way, the news can only be better than expected. And the policeman will have already come out with it.

Roxy waits for the moment of relief, but her husband is dead and after that there's nothing to be relieved about. She says, 'Well, come on in then.'

She doesn't like having strangers in the house. Half a day can be wasted on a washing-machine repairman. First there are the hours spent waiting for the stranger, then the house no longer belongs to her. When the man finally rings the bell and she opens the door, all the oxygen in the house escapes. She's friendly to the washing-machine repairman—cracking jokes, making coffee, smiling a lot. She pays and gives him an appropriate tip. But it all seems to take place under water; you can't keep it up for long.

'Sit down,' Roxy says. She points at the bar stools. The bar was her idea. Arthur gave her permission. Arthur doesn't like her saying he 'allowed' her to do something. The bar stools are for people who drop by, drink coffee for an hour and then leave. It's rare anyone stays an hour.

The policeman and woman sit down and now it's Roxy's turn to talk, cry, ask questions, maybe even scream. She wonders what they are expecting. She has reluctantly allowed these strangers in, but she understands this can't be dealt with quickly. She can't nod politely, say, 'thanks for the information' and rush them out the door—this is going to take time.

She hasn't realized she's been holding her breath; now she gasps for air. But the only thing that goes in is water, and she chokes on stifled tears.

She tries to say, 'I can't,' but of course she can and soon she is breathing in this world, just like the others. Okay, so this is going to take a while.

'I'll fetch my dressing gown.'

She goes upstairs and quietly enters her daughter's bedroom. The child is lying on her stomach. Roxy lays her hand on her daughter's back and waits until she can feel the life in the small body.

When she's back in the kitchen, she realizes she's forgotten her dressing gown.

'My dressing gown.' She goes back upstairs.

The younger of the two police officers—the woman—looks anxious. Roxy doesn't envy her.

'Have you had to do this before?'

The man nods.

'And you?'

'No.' The policewoman smiles and Roxy is grateful because it's the first time for both of them.

Their total lack of haste is remarkable; their calm says that everything has already happened.

'Now what?' She looks at the man.

'You can go to him ... see him. We'll take you.'

'He *is* dead, isn't he?' Roxy says, shocked, as though she hadn't understood and was actually supposed to be hurrying.

'Yes,' the man says, 'he's dead. He died on the spot and was taken to the hospital mortuary. We can take you there.'

'My daughter. She's sleeping.'

'How old is your daughter?'

'Three.'

'Can't you ask a babysitter to come? Family member?'

'My family live a long way away.'

'Neighbours?' She shakes her head and doesn't say that the girl next door, an economics student, picks up her daughter and babysits her practically every day. She even has a key. Although all three of them are breathing in the same space, they remain strangers, and naturally she lies to strangers. It doesn't occur to her to say she'd do anything except leave her daughter, wake her up, unsettle her.

'Do I have to go to the hospital?'

'Nothing's compulsory,' the man says.

'You have to call someone,' the woman says.

'It's late,' Roxy says. 'Everyone's in bed.'

'There are times when it's all right to wake people up. You have to call someone, madam.'

'All right.' Roxy looks outside. 'It's almost full moon.'

It's silent for a moment. Everyone looks outside and

the young policewoman says, 'Yes, almost.'

'You're the one who wrote that book, aren't you?' the man says.

Roxy knows which book he means. There's only one book people know—her first—but she can't resist saying: 'Which book? I've written three.'

'With the truck on the front.'

She nods.

'Fancy that,' he says.

'Do you want a drink?'

'We'll wait here with you until you've called someone.'

Roxy feels a rush of fear. 'You don't have to leave on my account.'

'Just make the call.'

'My phone's upstairs.'

'We'll wait here.'

She goes upstairs again. She doesn't know who to call in a situation like this. She can't think of anyone other than Arthur. She goes into their bedroom. The telephone is on her bedside table: she likes to have it within reach. She sits down on the bed, takes the phone and stares at it, a pointless thing now. She lets it slip through her fingers and waits until enough time has passed for her to have called someone.

She stands facing the two police officers in her kitchen. As soon as she says she's called someone they'll go. She shouldn't have lied about the babysitter. She shouldn't have been so silly about the book. The intruders have become her forsakers at an inconceivable rate of knots.

There's a business card on the kitchen table.

'Did you make the call?'

'Yes, my ... somebody ... somebody's coming.'

They get up.

'Won't you have a drink?' They could be friends.

'How did you meet?' people would ask later.

'Yes, it's an unusual story,' she'd say. 'They were the ones who came to tell me about Arthur's accident. They stayed the entire night afterward. They'd read my books—that was nice. We drank the wine that Arthur had stored right at the bottom of the rack in the basement, the expensive bottles.'

The man says, 'My colleague will come and see you again early tomorrow morning. Okay?'

'Okay,' Roxy says. 'Lovely.'

Roxy doesn't ask herself how you tell a three-year-old something like this—you just say it. She sits on the bar stool in the open kitchen and knows she'll have to wait until her daughter wakes up before she tells her. Louise has a father for one last night.

The counter is spotless. It's Wednesday; the cleaner has been. The espresso machine Roxy struggles with shines. All of this belongs to just her now. The house has become alien in one swift blow. They'd never owned it together: she'd lived in *his* house.

She mentally runs through her possessions, beginning with the kitchenware, then the furniture, the house, the car (the Camaro was a total write-off of course, but she still has the suv), the bank accounts. If you've never taken care of yourself, it's a scary mystery how you accumulate goods. It's inconceivable that you might have qualities, or be able to do things that people would pay good money for.

When she was seventeen, she left home carrying two weekend bags. She didn't look back. Arthur would be waiting around the corner to pick her up. It was a golden ticket that left no room for doubts. Arthur arrived twenty minutes after the agreed time. That wasn't right, she thought at the time. It was a bad sign. Like James Bond, she had to step from one flying aeroplane onto another—a perilous stunt but not impossible—but the plane you step onto can't coolly turn up twenty minutes late.

Twenty minutes of freefall on the corner of Saint Vitus Street and the Molenhof.

Ten years later she falls even further. She sits calmly on the bar stool at three in the morning, wide awake, searching for ideas, comparisons. She has spent years of her life sitting in her study pondering these kinds of metaphors. She can spend an entire afternoon working on a sentence and be happy. Although, on those tranquil afternoons, she has an increasing sense that she won't be able to get away with this much longer.

She has always known that she skipped something, took a short cut to adulthood. Now they're coming to get me, she thinks. Now I have to go back, and of course she doesn't call anybody. Not only to her daughter is Arthur not dead yet, but also to Roxy herself. Roxy is happy, one more night, one last hour.

The darkness does its work. She's lying in bed; she has turned off the light but her eyes are still open and she is afraid. She screams into her pillow so as not to wake her daughter.

Before she falls asleep, she hears the birds. She is awoken by her daughter's voice.

'It's morning,' Louise cries, 'the sun has risen!' It's a line she must have remembered from a story, a film. For the last few weeks, that strange, complete sentence has been coming from her daughter's bedroom: It's morning; the sun has risen.

THEY ARE IN the kitchen when Liza, the babysitter, lets herself in. It's Thursday, one of the days Arthur used to look after their daughter. Arthur insisted they share the childcare. He was proud that he was doing half of it, which meant that he arranged half of it. Liza came on his days with Louise.

'Good morning,' Liza says.

'Daddy is dead,' Louise says. 'We're eating pancakes.'

That morning she'd lifted her daughter out of bed, taken her into her own, and waited patiently until she was properly awake.

'Daddy working?' Louise was used to him being away a lot, yet she often asked after him.

'No,' Roxy said. 'I have to tell you something. Daddy is dead. He had an accident in the car and now he can't come back to us.'

The girl looked frightened and said, 'Don't be silly.'

The concept of death was brand new. She'd seen her father swatting flies—it had interested her. She'd wanted to look at the dead insects.

Later, she'd called out to her mother: 'I will make you

dead,' and when that had been forbidden, she'd tried again: 'You *are* dead,' but that wasn't allowed either. So on that morning, when her mother said that her father was dead, it was breaking all the rules.

Roxy said that it was true, honestly, and that you were allowed to say it. The child seemed to understand.

Then she asked, 'How do we make him alive again?' and Roxy had to say, 'We can't.' Louise cried, her mother rocked her, kissed away the tears, and Louise asked whether they were going to have pancakes.

Roxy stands behind her daughter, who is sitting at the bar in a child's high chair, trying to roll up a pancake.

'It's true,' she says. 'Arthur was in an accident.'

She strokes her daughter's head and talks like in a children's book. 'And now he's dead.'

The young student stares at Roxy and turns red; the news seems to have embarrassed her. Roxy's words are meant for her daughter.

'It's very bad,' she says, each word picked to take account of a three-year-old's mind.

'Last night the police came round—two of them. A policeman and a policewoman.' She almost says, *in blue uniforms.*

She manages to cobble together an appropriate adult sentence. 'It's beyond belief.'

'Jesus,' Liza says. 'Jesus.'

It's not that Roxy wants to protect her child from her grief. She knows that wouldn't be possible—it goes without saying.

Arthur wasn't convinced she'd make a good mother, and she'd shared his concerns. She'd never felt offended that he hadn't trusted her as a mother at the start, it all dovetailed so neatly with her own anxieties. For the past three years, she had observed with continuous amazement how easy she found it, adopting this role. But it remained a role—Daddy could intervene at any moment. Arthur had withdrawn slowly, he was around less and less. She became absorbed in the game with increasing dexterity. Today the game has become serious and she stands stiffly behind the child, stroking her hair incessantly.

'I must be in shock.'

'Of course.'

'The police will be here again shortly.'

'Jesus,' Liza says again. 'How terrible.'

'Yes.'

'Arthur ... Jesus ... What happened?'

'Louise, dear, do you want to watch television?'

The Smurfs DVD is still in the machine. Roxy selects the option PLAY ALL EPISODES. She closes the glass doors separating the living room from the kitchen so that they can talk without being disturbed.

Liza has sat down next to her. 'What happened exactly?' Roxy wants to reply but she doesn't know the answer.

'I forgot to ask.'

'But what did they say?'

'They're coming at ten o'clock.'

Liza is sitting there, all prepared, and now Roxy can't give her anything. She's got nothing at all to offer.

'It's not like me, you know,' she says, 'not asking. If someone's committed suicide I always want to know how they did it. Arthur doesn't. I get that it's inappropriate but I always want to look when there's an accident on the motorway. I wish I was the kind of person who didn't look. Arthur never looks but I can't help it. It's one of those things, like picking a scab. Do you look at traffic accidents?'

'No.'

'No?'

'No.'

They stare at the remains of the breakfast the way you look at the empty glasses after a party.

'And you don't know ... where?'

'No.'

'But where was he, then?'

'He had a premiere, in Utrecht, I think.'

'You *think*?'

'I think so, yes.'

Roxy has spent almost an hour now with the babysitter; they've never spent this long in each other's company before. She can't send Liza away, she has to be there later, when things need to be done and Louise can't be left on her own. She'll have to do things with strangers more often now; she'll need Liza for longer than just today.

'Have you called your family already? Yes, of course— or friends ... is anyone coming?'

'I haven't called anyone at all.'

'No one?'

'If I call people now they're going to ask all kinds of questions and I don't know anything yet, you see.'

'Don't you want to call anyone?'

'Sorry.'

'What for?'

'That I told you so ... first. It's too much, isn't it? It's too much for you. Of course, I should have called someone.'

'Should I take Louise?'

'Where to? What do you mean?' She sounds shocked.

'Do you want me to go out for a bit with Louise?'

'I'd rather she was here.'

'Do you want me to stay today?'

'Yes please. Is that okay?'

'Of course.'

They are silent but it no longer feels awkward. By asking her to stay, Roxy has made Liza seem less of a stranger.

Roxy lays a hand on her belly; her period came yesterday. 'I used to want seven children.'

'Really?'

'A long time ago, when I was a kid.'

'And now?' Liza blushes again.

'I'm still young.'

'Yes.'

'I'd forgotten about having wanted so many children. I only remembered it once Louise was born. As a child, I used to say it all the time and my mother would say, "You'll have to marry a rich man then, a doctor or something." Later I only remembered about having to marry a doctor but I'd forgotten why.'

'Should I call someone for you?'

'I'll wait until I know a bit more.'

Liza seems to want to say something about this but doesn't. She gets up and clears the kitchen table, carries the plates to the dishwasher. She knows her way around the house. She often does this when she's alone with Louise, but Roxy has never seen it. She doesn't come downstairs on those days.

'You've got a boyfriend, haven't you?'

'No,' Liza says, 'not anymore.' She remains at the counter.

'Did you break up?'

'Yes.'

'When?'

'Last month.'

'Was it bad?'

'So-so.'

'How long were you together?'

'Two years.'

'Fairly long.'

'And you?'

'Ten.'

'I think you should call somebody.'

Liza is wearing a floral wrap dress, the kind she'll be wearing in thirty years' time but then just below the knee rather than just above it, a respectable young woman who surely looks like her mother.

Roxy asks, 'How old are you, by the way?'

'Twenty-two.'

'Only five years between us. We could have been at school together.'

'We could have been at university together,' Liza says.

'I didn't go.'

'But it's possible. You still could.' Liza leans on the counter and then sits on it. Roxy imagines Liza's house, the flat the three students share, its unquestionably small kitchen and the way they cook together. No one has ever sat on their counter before.

'How did you meet, you and Arthur?'

'At a talk show. He'd just produced a major film.'

'And you'd written that book.'

'Yes.'

'You were really young,' Liza says.

'Too young to drive. My father took me to the studios

in Hilversum in his truck. They loved that—they all did.'

'He was a truck driver, wasn't he?'

'Still is.'

'International?'

'That too. That's what my book was about.'

'I haven't read it.'

'It's a trashy book.'

'My mother has.'

'The end,' Louise calls from the living room.

'A new one will start on its own,' Roxy shouts back.

Liza asks, 'Did you like him right away—Arthur?'

'I was mainly surprised that he liked me.'

'Why?'

'It was dreadful. After the broadcast, my father came up to us and began to tell a dirty joke.'

Silence.

'What are you thinking now?' Roxy asks.

'What was the joke?'

'Huh?'

'Can you remember it?'

'I'm no good at telling jokes.'

'But you do still remember it?'

'There's a hunter and he's trying to shoot a bear ... I really can't tell jokes.'

'Just tell it.'

'The hunter tries to shoot the bear but he misses and the bear says, "If you want to live you have to give me a blow job."'

She pauses for a moment and looks at Liza, but this time Liza doesn't blush. She smiles. 'Carry on.'

'Well, the hunter does it. Afterward he goes to the shop and buys a bigger gun. Back to the woods, misses again. The bear says again, "If you want to live you're going to have to give me a blow job." Blow job. Back to the shop, an even bigger gun, into the woods, misses again, blow job again ... When my father tells it, it goes on a lot longer.'

'Just carry on.'

'Fine,' Roxy says. She speaks louder. 'The guy leaves the woods again, swearing his head off, fucking this, fucking that, back to the shop and buys a bazooka. Now I'll get him. Goes back into the woods. All of a sudden there's a tap on his shoulder. He turns around; there's the bear again. The bear smacks the bazooka out of his hands.

'The bear says, "Hey, have you come here to hunt or to give me blow jobs?"'

Liza is grinning from ear to ear. They can hear the Smurfs singing in the living room and then Liza laughs out loud, just for a moment, and then Roxy is laughing too. She knows the joke from her father's telling it and later from Arthur too, but this is the first time it has made her laugh.

'It's quite good,' Liza says, and right away Roxy thinks that maybe Liza's dress isn't all that bad.

'My father could tell it better.'

'And Arthur? Did he like it?'

'Found it hilarious.'

'What was so dreadful then?'

'When anyone asks how we met, Arthur always tells that joke. Every time.'

'Romantic.'

'Yes. Three months later I'd moved in.'

'Were your parents pleased? Not a doctor, but rich anyway.'

'No,' Roxy says because her parents weren't pleased

and 'no', she says again, but that's a no to the no, that's not how it was. It wasn't like that. She'd always considered herself a rebel, a girl who ran away from home when she was seventeen, for a man who was thirty years older. Her parents hadn't spoken to her for three years, which had only contributed to the feeling she'd been rebellious.

Slowly they got back in touch and later it turned out that her parents had been following them all that time. They'd cut articles out of the literary supplements; they had first editions. Right from the start they'd kept a scrapbook of articles about Arthur's company, photos of the two of them at parties and premieres. Over recent years she'd been less in the news herself. The premieres began to bore her. There were always female friends or interns who appreciated going along instead and Roxy was just as happy to stay home. Just knowing she was his wife was enough for her. Her parents carried on cutting out articles but she no longer featured on the last pages of the scrapbook.

ROXY ASSUMES THE second visit will be a formality, something to do with paperwork, but the policewoman doesn't have a bag. She sits on the same stool at the bar again and doesn't put any papers on the table.

Liza has taken Louise upstairs. The policewoman said twice she really didn't want any coffee but Roxy insisted until she gave in.

Roxy says, 'I can't imagine you've had a nice cup of coffee at the police station already,' and she wonders out loud why the coffee is undrinkable in some places. She's never been to a police station but it sounds credible that the coffee would be bad there, and the policewoman doesn't say otherwise. Whenever Roxy enters the realm of small talk, she easily finds herself saying things she doesn't mean, has imagined, or couldn't possibly know. The melody of what she says is believable but the words themselves are nonsense.

She has to work the espresso machine herself now and with a witness at hand too. She presses the wrong button, amplifying her clumsiness: better a clumsy wacko who is surely brilliant at something else than just a regular klutz who can't even make coffee.

'I'm not very good with this machine.'

It occurs to her that the young policewoman is making little effort to converse with her.

'Have you slept?' is the only thing she asks Roxy, but it sounds like a medical intake question.

'I slept for three hours.'

The police officer nods.

'Do you think that's a lot or a little?'

The police officer doesn't reply.

'What's your name again?'

'Annemarie.'

Roxy copies all the actions she always saw Arthur do. The machine makes a racket; coffee trickles out. She's forgotten to warm the cups. She stops talking until the noisy machine has finished.

'I hope it's hot enough.' Roxy sets the coffee in front of the police officer, tastes her own and says, 'Not hot enough.'

The police officer says, 'Your husband wasn't alone in the car. Mariëlle Dupuis was with him.'

'The intern?'

'Yes, we understand she was his intern.'

'Oh God,' she says. 'And how ...?'

'She died in the ambulance.'

Of course, it's difficult for the death of a vague acquaintance to shock her any further but she allows the image of this death to sink in out of emotional politeness. She imagines the bits that broke, where she bled, a torn-off arm, a shattered skull. These things happen.

Arthur was dead on impact, which sounded clean-cut: painless and decent. Now she realizes you can die on impact and that your entire body can be broken. What did she say exactly—'on the spot'? Oh God, that wasn't the same as: 'on impact'. She only sees that now.

'Did he suffer?'

'We think he died instantly.'

'You didn't say that yesterday, did you? Yesterday you said, "on the spot."'

'Yes. He died at the site of the accident.'

'But when you arrived ...'

'He was already dead.'

'But in between the accident and you arriving?'

'We think he died instantly.'

'You *think* so.'

'Yes, we think so.'

'And were they together in the ambulance, when she died, or not? Dead people aren't allowed in ambulances, are they?'

'The fire brigade transported your husband.'

'They do that as well?'

'Yes.'

The fire brigade sounds bleaker than an ambulance; it sounds like tidying up. Suddenly she feels jealous of the young woman who died. She'll be mourned a lot more than Roxy's older husband. She thinks about Mariëlle's family, who are, of course, already at the hospital. Arthur is there alone. What is she still doing here?

'Did you have to go there last night too—to her family?' The policewoman nods.

Last night they seemed so united. It was the first time for both of them, a night like that. Only she knew she'd have to play the same tune all over again afterward. Of course she'd have had to watch how her colleague did it and then she'd be allowed to do the talking herself at the next visit.

'Why didn't you say so yesterday?' Roxy knows it's a

trivial question and there are a thousand more important questions to ask and that she'll ask them all many times: how, what time, how exactly, what was the fatal blow?

'But I was the first? I *was* the first, wasn't I, that you came to?'

'Yes.'

'You didn't go there beforehand?'

'No.'

'You can just say so, you know.'

'We went to see her family after you.'

'Does she have a boyfriend?'

'We spoke to her parents.'

'Did you stay there for a long time?'

Annemarie doesn't answer. She turns her cup of coffee around in her hands. She hasn't taken a sip yet; the coffee must be lukewarm by now.

'How old is she exactly?'

'Are you aware of the nature of the relationship she had with your husband?' The corner of Annemarie's mouth twitches nervously and Roxy knows this expression from when people expect her to be suspicious.

'I'm not jealous,' Roxy says. The policewoman searches for words. Roxy doesn't give her the chance to say anything.

'My husband ...' Roxy says, 'my husband is a flirt—a ladies man—I know that, of course. I'm the opposite. I don't have any male friends. I can't get on with them. The funny thing is that everyone always suspects him of cheating but he's quite the ...'

Roxy is unsure how far to go in her explanation to this woman she doesn't know, but it seems like the last time she'll be able to explain it to anyone, so a stranger will just have to do. She likes to talk about her husband. Most people don't understand him. She's often unhappy with the way they see him.

She says, 'My husband ...' she sits down, 'my husband had a very ...' she searches for the word, '*comfortable* ... relationship with sexuality. He wasn't afraid of it. He knew what he felt.'

She takes her time. She will build a modest monument of words for him.

'I have always admired that because I'm quite weak in those things. I have to shut myself off. I'm frightened when I'm attracted to other men. I like to keep my world uncluttered because I don't know how to cope with unwelcome feelings. Because I don't trust myself.'

She has only just begun. She laughs scornfully and assumes that the policewoman won't have understood, but something will seep through and later she'll think back to her words of wisdom.

'Arthur knew how far he could go. He knew himself. He trusted himself and I trusted him.'

The police officer looks at her coffee, cautiously raises her head and says, 'They were naked. The car was hit on the hard shoulder. They were found naked.'

Only now does it occur to Roxy that the word 'comfortable' wasn't right. As though she's sent reality down the wrong path with an ill-chosen word. She tries to come up with a plausible reason for the nakedness of her husband and the intern but doesn't get far.

Like the previous night, Annemarie has averted her gaze. Perhaps she understands that Roxy wants anything except to be seen. The officer doesn't watch her arrogant gaze dissolving and wretchedness growing inside her.

Roxy stands up, grabs the policewoman's coffee and empties the cup into the sink.

'It's cold,' she says. 'You mustn't drink that. Cold coffee's disgusting.' She turns on the tap and rinses the cup until all the coffee residue has gone, but the images aren't washed away with it: Arthur and the girl, naked in a car, mutilated bodies entwined; Arthur dying in a stranger's arms; her death cry. *The funny thing is that everyone always suspects him of cheating.* Will that line stay with her forever now?

Roxy thinks about her parents, about their scrapbook and the fact she's going to have to be the one to tell them. Even though she only sees them three times a year at the most, she seems to have become a child again all of a sudden, like she's in their house, and first she'll have to brave them taking in this scandal before she can take it in herself.

'Do her parents know this?'

'I believe her family went to the hospital last night and they've been told all the details.'

'Details,' Roxy says, imagining the details. 'Is Arthur … is he still in one piece?'

'He's in the hospital mortuary. You can visit him. The doctor there can give you all—'

'The details?'

'Yes.'

Roxy turns off the espresso machine, instantly giving up the notion of ever being able to use the thing and runs the tap again but the sink is clean. Would the bodies be carefully separated at the site of an accident like that, or might parts of one still be in the other?

'Stop picturing it,' Arthur always said if she got carried away in painful fantasies, like if she was watching unpleasant TV shows and crying. 'Don't do it,' he'd say. 'Why don't you turn off the television?' It had seemed to annoy him more and more in recent years, as though she was the person who had invented all the misery in the world. It was her own fault that she pictured it.

Roxy turns off the tap and lets the images work their way in, uncensored: his lustful hands stroking her young breasts, her mouth around his penis, his facial expression as he came, and the strange girl watching him at that moment. When you say it out loud it becomes more real, as though what is heard can no longer be denied. She turns to the policewoman.

'Was his penis still attached? Or is it inside her? Would that be possible?' Annemarie looks at her hands on the table; no more cup of coffee to stare at. Roxy doesn't want to shock her, that's not her point. She just wants to break Arthur's rules that state that people mustn't emphasize pain.

'Darling, anything you pay attention to only grows,' and Roxy gives her loved one and the strange young woman her full attention, exactly the thing he would try to dissuade her from doing. She has to do something, doesn't she?

She hears Louise running around and screaming upstairs and Liza calling her.

The police officer stands up and shakes Roxy's hand. She seems to want to say something and then realizes that there isn't anything she can say. Roxy doesn't let go. Holding Annemarie's hand in her own it's as though someone has played a malicious joke on them. Roxy continues to hold her hand and the policewoman allows it, until Louise comes downstairs, screaming with pleasure, and runs into the kitchen in her pyjamas. She breaks their covenant; the hands let go. Louise's joy cuts through the atmosphere in the kitchen like a knife. Liza runs after her saying she has to come back, she has to get dressed. Louise is enjoying the game and runs away until she sees the policewoman. She stops and stares through her white-blonde hair hanging in tangles in front of her face. She points.

'Police,' she says. She smiles blissfully, as though Mickey Mouse himself were in the kitchen. For a moment they are all silent and Roxy, too, looks at the shiny gold insignia on Annemarie's cap, the police emblem on her chest, the belt with holster and handcuffs.

'Yes, police,' Annemarie says. 'And who are you?' Louise says nothing.

'Her name's Louise,' Roxy says. 'This is Louise.' She lifts up her daughter and clutches her to her chest.

'Mummy,' she squeals.

'I'm going to flatten you,' Roxy says.

'Don't!' Louise cries as her mother relaxes her grip. 'Again!'

'If you've got any more questions you can always call us.'

Annemarie says she'll manage and excuses herself. Roxy clutches and releases her daughter, time and time again.

'Stop!' Louise shouts, and 'again', and 'stop', and 'again', until they're tired, until Roxy simply holds her child against her quietly, cheek to cheek.

'We're stuck together,' Louise says. Roxy carefully tries to pry her daughter loose but she presses herself harder into her mother.

The doorbell rings. Roxy doesn't move. Liza goes to the door.

It's Jane, Arthur's PA. 'Is he still asleep?' Roxy would recognize that deep, smoky voice anywhere. When she works upstairs and Arthur's PA comes round, she can hear it right away, a sonorous hum, even though she can't make out the words.

'Hi, darl', Jane says. 'Aren't you up in your attic yet?'

'Say hello,' Roxy says to her daughter.

'Say hello yourself,' Jane says. 'I was talking to you, hon.'

'Hello Jane,' Roxy says. Jane winks. In the distant past, Jane had been Arthur's driving instructor. Later she'd done something to do with purchasing art. She's got a girlfriend of Roxy's age whom Roxy has never met and who people say is stunning. Roxy doesn't know what impresses her the most about Jane, perhaps the fact she smokes like a trooper and isn't planning to stop.

Jane has actually retired; she started doing this on the side to help Arthur out of a tight spot after he'd fallen out with yet another assistant—a favour to a friend. Now she's been doing it for years.

'Otherwise I'd just get bored,' she says when people ask. Arthur believes he's doing her a favour. Roxy thinks the opposite.

'Where is that asshole?'

Liza nods toward Louise. 'Shall I take her upstairs again?'

Roxy says, 'I have a headache. I need coffee.'

Liza reaches out her arms to Louise but Roxy doesn't let her go.

'I just want a bloody normal coffee machine, something normal. What the fuck is wrong with just a normal coffee machine? I need to go to the mall.'

Jane points at the counter. 'Is the espresso machine broken?'

'It's a bugger,' Roxy says, walking to the kitchen carrying Louise. Liza follows them, as though she doesn't want to stay with Jane.

Roxy feels she shouldn't ask but she does anyway, 'Liza, would you—'

'Give her to me.'

'No, I mean ... will you tell her?'

Without waiting for a response, Roxy opens the door and leaves the house, still carrying the pyjama-clad Louise. She has left and she has everything she needs with her. It's funny how great the relief is, being out of the house she has only left reluctantly in recent years. She strides along the street taking enormous steps, her daughter bouncing up and down on her hip.

'Clip-clop, clip-clop,' Louise says, like a horse in one of her picture books. To Roxy, she seems lighter than ever.

In the hardware shop, she calls for the sales assistant: 'Sir!'

'Yes?'

'I want the cheapest coffee maker.' It mustn't look anything like their espresso machine.

'Come with me,' the man, whom she's never seen in the shop before, says. Maybe he's new, maybe he's the manager and isn't usually on the shop floor.

'All the coffee machines are here.' He opens a vitrine with a key. 'We've got this Philips one for €24.95: the jug turns into a Thermos flask so it uses less energy. Then we've got a Tomado for €15.95: quite a standard coffee maker, nothing fancy.'

'And that one?' She points.

'Yes, that's a little one: €9.95—perfect for a caravan or a student dorm.'

'Is it the cheapest one?'

'And then we've also got machines which grind the beans, but they're more sophisticated models.'

'I want the cheapest.' She just manages to say it in a friendly voice.

'Do you want the Tomado then? Or—?'

'That one.' She points again.

'You mean the little one?'

'It's the cheapest, isn't it?'

'Yes.'

'Yes.'

'Right, the little one then. I'll just fetch a boxed one from the back.'

Roxy goes to the till. There's a rack of Smurfs films, Smurfs glasses, and Smurfs pyjamas.

'Smurfs,' Louise says who loves to name things by their names. The man walks up with the coffee machine. Roxy strokes a pair of blue pyjamas with a Smurfs pattern.

'That'll be €9.95.'

'You like these?' she asks her daughter.

'Yes.'

They're pyjamas Roxy would have wanted herself as a child, only she wore long floral nighties and hand-me-down pyjamas from her older neighbours. Clothing with prints from television series was an unknown luxury, something that has remained unknown because in their household such things are considered tasteless. Their daughter wears tasteful little striped pyjama suits. Even the buttons are pretty, with little anchors. They suit her daughter, really, genuinely.

Roxy strokes the plastic Smurfs print, wonders whether it smells like plastic inflatable animals, and repeats her question: 'Do you like these?' She doesn't hear her daughter. She takes the pyjamas from the rack. 'And these.' Under the pyjamas featuring Brainy Smurf, there's a pair with Smurfette. She takes those too, 'and these'—and underneath is the big Smurf with the red hat, 'and these.' Under there's another pair with the big Smurf.

'Do you have any others?'

The man comes out from behind the till immediately, happy that he can help her with something.

'I believe there are also ones with Jokey Smurf,' he says, beginning to search the pile. When he's done, he searches through the pile again.

'No,' he says, 'we're out of Jokey Smurf.'

Roxy stands in front of her house, carrying her daughter in one arm, the shopping bag with the coffee maker and the Smurfs pyjamas in the other. It's no longer her house. She wants to reject it but it has already rejected her.

Her own mother joined a convent to escape her parents and married her father to escape the convent. None of this was unusual. In her circle, in those days, these were the usual options and none of it needed to turn out badly as long as you didn't choose the wrong convent and the wrong husband.

Roxy wants to escape now but Arthur has beaten her to it. There's nothing left for her to do.

She can't get to her key and doesn't want to put either her daughter or the coffee maker down. Inside are the two women who have been organizing their lives for the past few years—the babysitter and the PA—both of them hired by Arthur, of course. If it were up to Roxy she'd do everything herself. On the days her computer freezes, she considers buying a typewriter, anything to avoid having to ask strangers for help. Now she's standing at the door to her house, inside are the employees she has inherited—or are they acquaintances, friends? She doesn't know; they're Arthur's, not hers—everything is Arthur's. She rings the bell, like a visitor.

JANE HAS BEEN crying. She looks at Roxy, opens her arms but doesn't move from where she's sitting, like a giant flesh-eating plant that Roxy meekly heads for, without putting down her bag or her daughter first. Jane's arms close around them, a large package that is almost impossible to embrace. Louise buries her face in her mother's neck.

Roxy always limits her conversations with Jane, has done for years. She has managed to avoid ever saying anything very stupid to her. This is only possible if she goes up to her room after two sentences. Now she's standing in the woman's arms with her daughter, waiting until the woman has finished consoling them and wondering whether Jane knows about Arthur and the girl. Was Roxy the only one who didn't know? Anything is possible. When it suddenly turns out that you've been had, you've no idea of the extent of your been-hadness.

'I really need a coffee now.'

Jane lets her go and says, 'Let me do it.' She turns on the espresso machine and Roxy realizes that she may have a coffee maker now, but there aren't any filters. Bloody hell, shouldn't the shop assistant have thought of that?

'I've peeled an apple for you,' Liza says to Louise.

Everything around her is taken care of, as though Arthur had planned it. Someone like Roxy can't be left to her fate. Recklessly, you take your intern on the hard shoulder, but to be on the safe side, you hire an assistant and a babysitter so that you don't leave things unmanaged—all very rational. Arthur arranges things. Roxy finally puts Louise down; the child immediately crawls under the table.

Roxy says, 'Liza has peeled an apple for you—won't you come and sit down?'

'I'm sitting here.'

'You have to eat your fruit.'

'I'll eat my fruit here.'

Roxy squats, kneels, and then continues on all fours until she's sitting next to Louise under the high table, the big shopping bag between them. Liza passes the dish with the chunks of apple. Roxy takes it without looking at Liza. Now she's sitting under her kitchen table, feeding apple to her daughter, like a child whose tortoise is eating out of her hand.

'It's nice having such a high table,' Roxy says to her little pet, 'then I can fit under it too.' It's the first time the high bar she wanted has come into its own.

'Is Daddy coming too?' Louise asks.

'No, Daddy's not coming because Daddy's dead, remember?'

'How do we make him alive?'

'We can't.'

'I want Daddy back,' Louise says, crying for the second time that morning.

'Yes,' Roxy says, 'I know.' She takes her daughter on her lap and rocks her, her hand on the small forehead, their cheeks touching, her daughter's tears running over her own face, until Louise frees herself and takes the pyjamas out of the bag.

'Which pyjamas do you want on?'

'Smurfette,' Louise says.

'Take everything off.' Roxy doesn't have to press her—Louise loves being naked.

'Roxy?' She jumps when she hears Jane's voice. She'd forgotten the women above her for a minute.

There's a standard line under all of Arthur's emails: 'My assistant, Jane Muller, will contact you shortly.' He didn't delete the text when he sent private things: photos, jokes, obscene messages. Once he'd written, 'I'm going to lick you out when I get home,' with, right under it in italics: *My assistant, Jane Muller, will contact you shortly.*

'Your coffee,' Jane Muller says. Roxy holds out a hand and takes the coffee. The cup is hot. Jane is a good PA: she's warmed it up.

'Roxy?'

She pretends not to hear Jane.

'Roxy?'

My assistant, Jane Muller, will contact you shortly.

Louise has already taken off her pyjama bottoms and underpants but her head gets stuck when she tries to take off the top without undoing the buttons.

'You have to open the buttons.' Roxy helps Louise until she's naked. She pulls off the cards on the Smurfs pyjamas but when Louise realizes that Roxy wants to dress her again, she quickly crawls out from under the table so she can stay naked. She runs into the hall. Roxy comes out from under the table too.

'What can I do?' Jane asks. 'Shall I come with you? Is

anyone going to go with you? Shall I call someone?'

'Where are we going then?'

'To Arthur?'

'Oh?'

Jane looks at the Smurfette pyjamas in Roxy's hand. 'What's up?'

'Mariëlle was in the car as well.' Jane knows her better than she does.

'The intern?'

'Mariëlle Dupuis. Yes.'

'And she's—?'

'Dead too.'

Liza groans, very quietly. 'Shall I take Louise upstairs for a bit?'

Louise hears her name and shouts from the hall: 'Not getting dressed!'

Jane sits down on a bar stool. 'Christ.'

'"Are you aware of … the nature of your husband's relationship with her?" The policewoman asked this morning … And you? Are *you* aware of the nature of Arthur's relationship with her?'

'What do you mean?'

'They were naked; they were found naked. Naked and dead,' Roxy laughs inanely and glances at Liza who is suddenly blushing again. Roxy says, 'Stupid, isn't it?' as though a child had done something clumsy.

'The bastard,' Jane says.

Louise runs into the kitchen. 'You're not allowed to say "bastard."' Roxy holds up the pyjamas causing Louise to run away again. Liza's red face hurts Roxy as much as her own shame does. Liza is young; she must think they're a right pair of losers. She never wants to be like that. Roxy sees in her all the disappointment that she can hardly get under control herself. It is this young, shocked face that gives her the courage to look at Jane, whom she wishes a long, happy life, and she notices that Jane's eyes are green.

LIZA HAS TAKEN Louise outside. Roxy wasn't able to prevent it.

She'd almost gone with them but Jane said, 'I'll help you with things here,' and Roxy thought, *I guess I'm staying here then.*

She is perched on the counter, like she saw Liza doing. Jane has her telephone and paperwork in front of her on the kitchen table.

'I don't want to see him,' Roxy says.

She waits until Jane says, *but of course not, I understand, of course you don't want to see him.* But Jane says nothing for way too long, until finally she says, 'You shouldn't if you don't want to.'

'Do I have to go and identify him, or how does that work?'

'I'm assuming they can get round that.'

'They can't force me to?'

'I don't think so, no.'

'What happens?'

'I don't know either.'

'But what do you think?'

'I don't know, Roxy. We'll have to ask.'

'Yes.'

'Have you got the address of … where he is?'

Roxy points at the card on the kitchen table.

Jane moves seamlessly from being Arthur's assistant to being Roxy's assistant.

'I'll make a list of everyone we have to call.'

Their social circles are jotted down in Jane's handwriting. An R or a J appears after each name. Jane can call unless Roxy really has to do it herself. It's amazing how infrequently her initial appears on the list.

Roxy has got one friend of her own age, Marco, a poet who shares the same publishing house. Marco is gay; he could never have become her friend otherwise. Roxy only knows one route with heterosexual men, the path to seduction, which is why she keeps them at arm's length.

Apart from Marco, she doesn't have any real friends. As an excuse she usually brings up the fact that most of the people around her are older which makes it difficult to make friends. But Roxy doesn't want any friends. Not needing them is a way of being special that she is particularly attached to. Arthur was enough for her, and for quite a while Arthur was happy with that, being somebody's only one.

Roxy doesn't feel at all like calling Marco, but she knows she'll be insulting him if she doesn't tell him today. In friendships, you have to hit the right degree of intimacy: you can insult your friends by not telling them enough. Marco offered himself up as a friend and stayed one. Roxy never understood why—she doesn't have much to offer.

It's a pity there's no discussion about which letter

comes after her parents' names. Before Roxy can speak up, Jane has already written an R.

'Bloody hell,' her father says, and again, 'Bloody hell,' and, 'I'll call your mother. Celia … Celia!'

Roxy hears him shuffling through the house in his Swedish clogs. She can smell their house, the dog, her mother's menthol cigarettes.

Her father has been home more in recent years; he hasn't got enough work. He's a self-employed driver but depends on her mother, who passed all her exams during her good years, to help run his company. Without a partner with a professional qualification, her father can't do anything. Even now, her mother still does the admin, and even though she spends much of the time drunk and in no fit state, when she's sober she's ten times more intelligent than he. They can barely stand each other's company but he has to stay with her so he can go off in his truck from time to time.

'Has Dad already told you?' she asks when her mother comes on the line.

'You poor thing.'

'Yes. Yesterday. Accident.'

'Yes, he just said.'

Roxy almost starts crying. She hears her own faltering breath.

'Oh baby.'

'Yes.'

'Should we come?'

'I don't know.'

'Just say.'

'I've got stuff to arrange.'

'Yes, I suppose you do.'

Then she hears her father ask, 'Is she coming to live here?' as though the whole life she'd built with Arthur had been just a minor detour.

'I'm talking, all right?' her mother says.

The dog barks. 'Quieten down, boy.'

'Oh yes,' Roxy says, 'you might read something in the papers about a girl or woman who was in the car with him.'

'Oh baby, they write so much. It's all just sour grapes.'

'Yes, but this time it's true. Just so you know.'

'Oh no, oh dear.' Roxy pictures her mother gently stroking the dog.

'What?' her father asks.

'Tell you in a minute.'

'What, then?'

Her mother tries to cover the mouthpiece but Roxy can still hear them. 'He was seeing someone else.'

'I knew it.'

It's boiling hot. Roxy is sitting under an enormous parasol on the patio in front of the conservatory. Marco turned up uninvited after her phone call, bringing with him Italian sandwiches, and cigarettes. Roxy isn't eating but she is smoking. Marco eats his own sandwiches and lets her recount the past twelve hours in detail. She can't deny that his presence is pleasant and asks, 'Why don't we do this more often?'

She hasn't heard the bell. All of a sudden she hears Jane saying her name.

'No, I'm not Mrs. Rombouts. That's Mrs. Rombouts.'

A big man is standing next to Jane in the kitchen and Jane points at Roxy.

'Roxy,' she says, 'the undertaker.'

'Oh,' Roxy says. She holds up a hand, 'hi.'

The man walks toward her. He looks like a removals man, big and strong, as though he has to carry the coffins himself. He shakes them both by the hand.

'I'm Hendriks. Please accept my condolences.'

Marco seems to be getting ready to go but Roxy insists he sit back down. She lights up new cigarettes for the two of them.

Jane and the undertaker are already sitting at the table with paperwork in front of them.

'Shouldn't you go inside?'

'What do you mean?'

'You're the widow.' Marco says it without irony.

She seems tipsy from all the coffee, cigarettes, and lack of sleep, giggles at the word 'widow' and says, 'Arthur and Jane are my parents. I'm the daughter.'

'And Louise?' Marco asks. 'Who's Louise?'

'Louise is my doll.' Now she really has to laugh. She looks into the kitchen and catches Jane's eye; her expression is far from loving. Marco quickly kisses her goodbye and whispers, 'Go on, I'll call you later. I'll see myself out.'

Roxy sits down next to Jane and strokes the plastic folders in an open ring binder with pictures of coffin handles.

She tries to sound serious. 'Copper looks nice.'

'We're not there yet,' Jane says.

'Sorry,' Roxy says. 'Where are we?'

She has to concentrate, go with the flow, know what is expected of her and give the impression of having an opinion about the colour of the coffin, the material the handle is made of, whether to have flowers or not, and all that at the appropriate moments. *Will not participate*, her favourite option in many areas of life, is not an option here. If she doesn't want to be told off like a child, she'll have to stop acting like one.

'You're the writer of that book,' Mr. Hendriks says later. The ring binders are already shut, but he hasn't finished his coffee yet.

'Yes, I am,' Roxy says charitably, and, 'How nice that you know that,' and then, 'You don't have to call me Mrs. Rombouts. Roxy is fine.' It comes out so smoothly, as though she's just learned manners and is cheerfully applying them for the first time, and wonder of wonders, it turns out not to be that difficult after all.

'I'll show you out.'

She watches him leave, walk down the street; his car is around the corner. He was on his way home, he said. She'd have liked to walk with him. Where does a man like that go? What kind of a kitchen does he have? She's convinced he doesn't have an espresso machine. He'd heard of her book.

Roxy doesn't like her debut: a hilarious yet tragic road novel about a trucker who takes his thirteen-year-old daughter along with him during the school holidays so she doesn't have to spend the summer with her alcoholic mother. It was poorly written but a good story and she was so young people forgave her everything. Full of promise.

When Arthur rescued her from the world which had earned her so much acclaim amongst readers who didn't know that world, she just wanted to get out as quickly as possible. She wanted nothing more to do with it.

In the large attic room Arthur furnished for her, she wrote hesitant, anxious stories which few people enjoyed reading. She'd written *The Trucker's Daughter* in five weeks, but in her attic room she could spend two months puzzling over the phenomenon of 'falling', end up with a single sentence and be happy.

She no longer wanted to be anywhere other than in her perfectly styled attic, far from the ground floor. The tough, angry child she was, was tucked into a large, soft bed. She became softer with the years but also more fearful. Slowly she began to worry that this was the only safe place on earth.

Arthur took care of her during the early years with an unearthly devotion. He was like a boy who had found a wounded, stray dog. But you mustn't lock away frightened dogs in comfort; they only become more frightened. Nice one, Arthur—now Roxy would be kicked out onto the street where, undoubtedly, she'd be met with loud jeers.

She is standing in the doorway now, delaying returning to the kitchen where Jane is waiting for her. Their road is dissected by a median strip with large shrubs. After a previous spot of bother, a photographer had stood there. Arthur's words, 'a spot of bother', a disagreement with a director who had accused Arthur of plagiarism.

'You don't need to get involved.' Of course she hadn't got involved.

Jane's telephone rings but she doesn't pick up.

'Some days he'd call me three times an hour and on other days I couldn't get hold of him,' Jane says. 'I'd spend the day calling everybody and saying, "I'll consult Mr. Rombouts," but really I already knew what Arthur wanted.'

'Yes.'

'You just think: what would Arthur want?'

'And you're good at that.'

'I think I was better at knowing what Arthur wanted than he did.'

'Couldn't you have given me a quick ring too?'

Jane laughs reluctantly.

'You knew?'

'No. I suspected it, but ...'

'But?'

'I thought he told me everything.'

'Maybe it was the first time,' Roxy says. 'Maybe he didn't normally do things like that.'

Jane remains silent.

Roxy says the intern's last name as though she has a nasty taste in her mouth, 'Dupuis. That's the one with the curly hair, isn't it?'

'Yes.'

'Are they real curls?'

'I've called her parents.'

'They weren't on the list.'

'It seemed appropriate.'

'What did they say?'

'Thank you.'

'Mr. and Mrs. Dupuis. What kind of people are they?'

'They own a pet shop.'

'Nice.'

'Here, in the city.'

'Dupuis Pet Store?'

'Total Animal.'

'Total Animal?'

'That's what it's called.'

'Do they have any other children?'

'No.'

'Fucking hell.' Roxy is crying. 'Fucking hell, I can't start crying about them!' but Roxy is crying. 'How could he do that?' She wipes away her tears. 'Total Animal.'

'Yes. It's in Zuid.'

'Shut up. I don't want to know.'

Jane gets her cigarettes out of her bag and goes into the conservatory.

'Jane,' Roxy calls out. 'Tell me one thing, just one thing ... that's better about me than her!'

Jane slowly lights her cigarette.

'Too late,' Roxy says.

'Roxy ...'

'Leave it.'

'Roxy, this won't help.'

'Too late.'

ON THE AFTERNOON of the funeral, Liza takes Louise to the paddling pool in the park. They'll join Roxy after the funeral. They leave through the back gate to avoid the photographers. The newspapers hadn't taken long to find out, but it only affects Roxy today. Now she has to go out and people will see her.

Jane comes to collect her. She is wearing a beige summer suit with Italian loafers. She is beautiful. Roxy is still wearing the same T-shirt and shorts she's been walking around in all week.

'You have to get dressed.'

'I haven't opened the wardrobe yet. All of our clothes are hanging there together.'

'You really will have to get dressed though.'

'I don't feel like seeing his clothes.'

'You're telling me that now? We only have half an hour.'

'Let them start without us.'

'Roxy, come on.'

'Will you come with me? To get dressed?'

'Hurry up then.'

It's an exciting thought: getting dressed with Jane

there—just enough of a distraction to be able to do it without crying, without drama.

Roxy throws the dirty laundry off the armchair in the bedroom. 'You can sit there.'

She opens the wardrobe doors. His suits take up half of the space. The smell of his aftershave is unmistakable, mixed in with a vague tinge of sweat and cigars. Her heart beats faster. Then she looks at Jane and takes off her T-shirt. She imagines Arthur seeing them, his shy young wife, half-naked in front of his PA.

Despite the heat, she puts on nylon tights, a pencil skirt, which makes it hard to breathe, a long-sleeved blouse; as much of her skin as possible is hidden. She chooses the highest heels, evens out her complexion with foundation, lips purple, everything just a little less human.

She looks at Jane in the mirror. 'Thank you.'

Jane nods. 'You're welcome.'

Jane hesitates at the door, the car keys in her hand.

'Do you want to go via the back door?'

Roxy picks up her sunglasses. 'No.'

Arthur has a lot of friends, colleagues, and acquaintances, so she won't be able to avoid the large-scale nature of the event, but it is an event, with a start and a finish time, a demarcated appearance and as far as she is concerned, it has already begun.

'We'll take the SUV. I'll drive.'

'Can you drive in those shoes?'

'Clogs, flip-flops, slippers ... I can drive in any shoes.'

'I couldn't even walk in those.'

Jane leads the way. The SUV is at the end of the street; they walk fast. All of a sudden, Jane stops.

'What is it?'

'There aren't any photographers.'

Roxy takes off her sunglasses and looks around. 'No.'

She sounds disappointed and can hear it in her own voice. There are many ways of being ridiculous and Roxy suspects she's just at the beginning of a long series of them.

Once she's behind the wheel she feels better, even though she hates this car. She should have gone for a drive right after his death.

'It's a stupid car, of course.'

'Yes.'

'Do you have to go to her funeral too?'

'Can't.'

'It's today?'

'Yes.'

'Did you send flowers?'

'Why do you want to know?'

'So you did.'

'You're driving too fast.'

'Do you think I should send something too?'

'Why should you? They haven't sent you any flowers.'

'Haven't they?'

'I don't believe there are any guidelines on this.'

Roxy brakes for a painter's van that is trying to back into a street. She gives it some space. The driver holds up a hand. Roxy nods. The orchestrated communication on the road always makes her melt; she feels a glimmer of love for other people. Not something she can use today.

'Idiot,' she says. 'He can't turn.'

'It's tricky.'

'That Volvo of yours has a small turning circle, I'm always surprised, such a large car. This one doesn't; it's a monster.'

'You're really embarrassed by your car, aren't you?'

'I don't mind if you send those people something from me.'

'Those people?'

'The parents.'

'You can do it yourself.'

'Is it a strange thing to ask?'

'We need to talk about my job description at some point.'

'Did you buy my birthday present from Arthur last year?'

'The cashmere scarf?'

'Yes?'

'Of course not.'

'What did you get, then?'

'Nothing. I didn't do those kinds of things.'

'Why did you ask if I meant that particular scarf, then?'

'I thought it was pretty.'

'Do you want it?'

'Arthur gave it to you.'

'It's ugly. You can have it.'

Roxy's father's old Scania is in the large car park at the back of the cemetery. Roxy draws in next to it. She'd told her parents they'd be better off coming straight here; they wouldn't be able to park their truck in Roxy's street.

Her mother is sitting on the steps, smoking; her father is standing a few feet away. They've brought the dog with them: a small, fat black thing of indeterminate breed, with short legs. When Roxy left home her father gave her mother the dog. Later he told her she'd complained about having to look after that filthy animal while he went happily on his way. She didn't even give it a name; she called it 'The Dog' but took better care of it than she ever had done of Roxy.

Roxy and Jane walk up to them. It takes them a while to react.

'Roxy?' her father says. 'Bloody hell, I didn't recognize you.' Her mother gets to her feet. She has become skinnier; she's shaking. Roxy kisses her cheek. Her mother was always a head shorter than her, but now she's wearing high heels, she feels like a giant confronting a quivering bird. Her father holds out his hand.

Jane introduces herself and condoles them on the loss of their son-in-law.

'Did you know him too?' her mother asks.

'Jane is Arthur's assistant,' Roxy says. 'They've known each other for more than twenty years.'

'A tragedy,' her father says, which sounds funny in his soft, southern accent. As often is the case, Roxy is surprised by how handsome her father is, leaving aside his enormous beer belly. He talks so much rubbish and he dresses so dreadfully, it's easy to forget his charm.

The dog sniffs around her legs. Roxy tries to push it away without showing her dislike of it. She looks absurd next to her parents, with her sunglasses and high heels.

'That's a pricey piece of kit,' her father says.

Roxy takes off her glasses. Her father looks past her, at the suv next to the Scania.

'Is it one of those fake Chevys,' he asks, 'the kind Daewoo make?'

'Yes.'

'Didn't expect to see you in one of them.'

'This one was Arthur's.'

'It's a decent vehicle.'

'Do you think so?'

'I liked that gold Nissan too. That was fancy.'

'Yes, that was a nice car.'

'But much smaller.'

'It wasn't big for an suv.'

'No, not for an suv.'

'But it was more than ten years old or something.' She immediately regrets saying this.

'Yes,' her father says to Jane, 'every time the ashtray was full, they'd get a new one!' He finds his joke very funny.

'Do you always take the truck when you go anywhere?'

'I've got an old Daffy at home, one of those old bone-shakers. Remember them?'

Her mother says, 'Shut up about cars, our baby's just lost her husband,' and they stop talking.

The car park is filling up. Roxy puts her glasses back on. 'I'm not sure if the dog's allowed inside.'

Her mother crouches next to the dog. 'He wouldn't hurt a fly.'

'Yes,' her father says, 'just like its owner.' Again he laughs at his own words.

'We have to go in.' Jane is already on the move.

'Go on. We'll join you in a minute.'

'Are you sure?'

'Yes, go on. Really.'

Her father watches Jane go. 'Is she a lezza?'

'Please, Gerard.'

'Aren't I allowed to ask?'

'Where's Louise?' her mother asks.

'She's coming after the funeral.'

Her father wipes his forehead with a hanky. 'I'm sweating like a pig.'

'Why don't you two go in?'

Her mother says, 'I don't know anybody.'

'Have you been here for long?'

''bout an hour.'

'Your mother didn't want to be late.'

Roxy wants to say something nice, remembers that Jane often uses the handy American expression 'I appreciate that', so she says that in Dutch and immediately hears how formal it sounds. She lays a hand on her mother's arm.

Her mother asks, 'Are a lot of famous people coming?'

Roxy has never really hated her parents; shame was the worst thing she felt. Her mother once picked her up from school—she never normally did—Roxy must have been around seven or eight. She stood smoking at the gate in a summer dress; it was autumn. Roxy was shocked. She ignored her mother and walked past her. They didn't mention it at home and she never did it again.

Her mother tries to hug her, but she is too short so Roxy has to stand strangely bent over in her arms. The dog barks.

'Down, boy,' her father says.

She sits at the front between her parents and Jane. The dog is lying under her mother's chair, panting incessantly because of the heat.

Arthur's older brother, an accountant from Zwolle, recollects their youth. Jane talks about their friendship, and Roxy pays no attention. It's not her party. She has often imagined Arthur's funeral: he was thirty years older than her. It was inevitable she'd experience it one day. She even knew what she'd say. It was horrible but it was hers at least—her party.

She is relieved when they've finished and she can move again. Roxy walks close behind the coffin and her parents shuffle along behind her with the dog.

She misses Arthur; it's a dirty trick, leaving her to fix this on her own. Immediately, she corrects herself internally, not because it would be impossible for him to support her at his own funeral but because it's impossible to miss him now. The person she is missing seems to have never existed. Over the past week, he has turned into a stranger and the woman who was with him seems just as unfamiliar to her: a stranger she no longer needs.

She watches the clumsiness with the coffin calmly, the way the men lower him into the ground using ropes. Roxy has no choice but to stay standing, with so many spectators around her, people she hardly knows who look at the betrayed widow with her shabby parents standing behind her and a dirty old dog. Even if she wanted to, she couldn't cry. She doesn't believe it's a question of honour because honour sounds so light, so frivolous, and what she feels is hard and cold, like hatred, but perhaps she should consider honour again and she thinks about her study, her refuge that will no longer be one. She throws soil onto the coffin with a steady hand. The other people's gazes are what make her so hard.

Usually, a gravel path is a difficult surface for these shoes but not today. Rarely has she walked so confidently on her high heels as at her husband's funeral.

The bar is open. This is what Arthur would have wanted, according to Jane. There's a sudden shaky moment because protocol fails at this point and she doesn't know where to go, whom to stand with, like at break time at school. Her father walks toward her with Marco at his side.

'Marco, this is my dad.'

'Yes,' Marco says, 'we've already had a chat.' Her father grins.

'Where's Mum?'

Her father points at the bar. 'I'm the designated driver.' He's been saying this for years and it's ridiculous because her mother doesn't even have a driving licence. He laughs and says even more loudly, 'I'm always the driver, right?' before slapping Marco on the shoulders.

The famous actors at the table on the other side of the auditorium look up. Roxy stands between them and her father and feels it would be impossible for her to bridge this gulf; it's too big. The bridge is Arthur and if you take Arthur away from her there's nothing left: a girl of seventeen who stopped existing long ago. Roxy stares at the people and finds it hard to imagine that they can see her. Someone clutches at her leg.

'Mummy.'

Her non-existent arms lift up her daughter. Roxy clamps Louise to her body. As long as she's holding her, she's got arms.

Liza has got changed and is wearing a black dress, for the first time, without a floral pattern.

'Hey you little scamp!' her father says to his granddaughter. Louise hides her face in Roxy's neck.

'Do you remember your Grandad?'

'You're frightening the child.' Her mother. 'Come to Grandma.' Louise presses herself closer to her mother but Grandma says, 'Look at this.' She's holding a lolly in one hand and a glass of sherry in the other. Louise lets go.

A waiter carrying a tray does the rounds. Roxy shakes her head. The waiter isn't bad looking but there's something inane about him. Roxy can't help weighing up all the men she used to ignore now. The waiter looks at her for longer than necessary and Roxy thinks, *it's inevitable then*. A dull feeling of resignation comes over her, as though she's already married to the idiot.

Her father lays a hand on Liza's shoulder, the way he does with his friends and asks, 'What's the difference between a penalty taken by the Dutch team and a glass of beer?'

Marco smiles.

'Don't say anything!' her father says.

Roxy tugs Marco outside by his arm and says she has to smoke.

'Yes,' Marco says, 'he is a very unusual man.'

'Who?'

Roxy bursts out laughing and then realizes that Marco wasn't joking. 'You meant that?'

Marco points at the truck. 'Is that the one?' He walks over to it; she follows reluctantly.

'That's touching,' he says when he sees that R O X Y has been written on it in large letters.

'There's nothing moving about that,' she says. 'He only put it on there when my book was successful.'

'So what?'

'He didn't speak to me—so touching. The coward. And meanwhile, showing off with my name.'

She sounds heartless; she'll lose Marco like that.

'*Your* name?'

'Stupid,' Roxy says. 'I always thought it was my name, but of course it belonged to him more than to me.'

'I think your dad's a very genuine man.'

'Why? Because he's not ashamed of anything? Is it that simple?' Marco suppresses his irritation. She's a new widow, after all.

'Come on,' she says, 'let's go and crack jokes with my dad. You'd like that, wouldn't you?'

'It's only because he's a bit of a rough diamond. He can be genuine.'

Roxy shouts, 'Bullshit!'

Marco's gaze becomes pitying. 'Come here.' He spreads his arms; now she has to walk over to him.

She remembers the few times she went to the pub with her father when she was young. Unlike her mother, her father never drank alone. He sometimes forgot she was there in the pub, but when she threatened to get angry, he'd notice her, spread his arms and shout out, 'Come to daddy.' The problem wasn't that she didn't want to, it was how to walk across the entire room on her way to his lap without losing face.

Louise is no longer with Roxy's mother. There's a woman next to her mother who Roxy doesn't know.

When she gets closer, she hears her mother saying, 'It's more fictional than people think.'

'Mum.'

'I'm talking to a friend of yours.'

'Hi,' the woman says. 'Clara.' She shakes her hand. 'Condolences; we've met before, at the office.'

'Yes.'

'I was just saying that your book is dramatized, as it were,' her mother says. These are the words she uses when she's doing her best to show people she's not trash. It's difficult to know what embarrasses Roxy more: her mother's sorry attempts or her father's ham-fistedness.

'Where's Louise?'

'She went off with that lesbian woman.'

'Please don't call her that.'

'Isn't she a lezza then?' Her father has come over to them.

'Her name's Jane.'

'Yeah, that one. She's a lezza, isn't she?'

'Gerard, please.'

Roxy looks for Jane in the crowd and tries not to make eye contact with anybody.

Louise is sitting on the floor at Jane's feet, making patterns with peanuts.

'You were supposed to stay with Grandma.'

'Grandma was being weird.'

'Was she any trouble?' Roxy asks.

'Louise?'

'My mother.'

'I don't have a problem with your mother.'

'But?'

'Sorry,' Jane says, 'but I'm not good with people like your father.'

'Thank God. I was afraid that he was going to be able to get everyone to burp the alphabet with him.'

Jane laughs, Roxy too. It's the first time they've both found something funny.

Then Roxy notices the row of people standing in front of her. She can't stop one person from shaking her hand and after that she finds herself standing there politely accepting condolences.

'Thank you, thank you, yes, thank you, yes, it's erm ... a lot, thanks, thank you, you too, yes, you've known each other for a long time, right?'

There are pretty actresses in the queue. Roxy can't stop herself from wondering whether they've been to bed with Arthur. Out of the corner of her eye she sees the waiter again. He is looking at her too.

She smells a familiar sweaty odour, turns around and her father is standing behind her. He whispers in her ear, 'You can do better than that, lass,' and now she is forced to laugh at him all the same.

HER MOTHER LOOKS happy. Less than an hour ago, Roxy said goodbye to her parents, promising to come visit them in Brabant soon and now here they are on her doorstep.

'I know you don't want this,' her mother says, 'that's why we are saying it, and not asking.'

'It was her idea.' Her father stands a foot behind her, ready to leave again if they're not welcome.

'We're here for you.' Her mother is still smiling and looking anxious all the same.

'What about the truck?' Roxy asks, almost believing her own lie that trucks don't fit down her street.

'Not a problem,' her father points toward the end of the street, where the truck is neatly parked.

'Who is it?' Jane calls out.

'Mum and Dad.'

Marco is already at her side. 'Hey, cool, man.' He gestures for her father and hugs him. Roxy has never seen anyone hug her father. The dog barks.

'Down boy, down boy,' her father says.

Liza is on the telephone. 'Hang on,' she waves coquettishly at Roxy's parents and shouts, '… extra pizza?'

'Lovely,' her father says.

'Do you eat meat?'

'He certainly does,' her mother says.

All the stools at the kitchen table are taken. Louise is lying under the table with the dog. The pizzas are shared out, swapped, and discussed. Roxy's mother shows friendly concern and asks Liza about her studies. For a moment, she's the woman she'd wanted to be.

'Celia? Where does that name come from?' Liza asks politely.

'Cecilia. Everyone called Cecilia gets called Celia.'

'You're not a Cecilia,' her father says, 'you're a real Celia.'

Her mother has put a new bottle of wine on the table and fills everyone's glasses.

Roxy can't help herself from counting and registering how much faster her mother drinks than the others.

Her mother's questions and answers become simpler, her reactions shorter, from 'oh yes,' to 'mmm,' and by the next bottle she is only nodding, until there's nothing but a vague smile left.

Roxy stands up. 'I'll go make up the guest bed.'

On the stairs, Roxy thinks: *I want to die.* But that's nothing new. Even in happier times, she'd wake up in the night and those words would be there, without any obvious cause. She has begun to consider them an irritating but not unsettling error, like a typo.

She puts clean sheets on the large guest bed; there are footsteps on the landing.

'Here!' Roxy calls out.

Her mother comes into the guest bedroom. They don't

look at each other. She sits down on the bed and takes off her shoes.

'Yeah girl,' she says.

'Yes,' Roxy says, 'you could say that.'

Marco has reached out across the kitchen table and is holding her father's hand. Liza is sitting next to Marco, leaning forward, totally engrossed in her father's story. He is sniffing and has watery eyes. Jane is smoking in the conservatory.

'The older you get, right,' her father says, 'the more those things bother you.'

'What things?'

'He's telling us about his little brother,' Marco says.

'I'm talking about wee Barry.'

'Oh, Barry,' Roxy says. 'I'm off for a smoke.'

In the conservatory, she sits in the chair Arthur always sat in. Jane is sitting in hers. They look through the glass doors into the kitchen.

'Is your father crying?' Jane asks.

Roxy has a good look. 'Yes, I believe so.' She lights up a cigarette and sinks into her chair. Jane stares ahead.

'What?'

'What are they talking about?'

'Oh, it's about his dead brother, just a baby. He had ... I can't remember what it was exactly, but Dad's good at telling the story. The child had two illnesses and you had to be kept warm for one of them and cold for the other.'

'And then?'

'And then he died.'

'How old was your father?'

'About two or something—very young. He can't remember any of it, yet he tells it beautifully—actually better and better—and the older he gets, the worse he finds it.'

Her father calls out, 'Roxy, is The Pump still open?'

Roxy opens the connecting doors. 'The Pump?'

'That pub on the corner we went to when Louise was born.'

'I didn't,' Roxy says. 'You might have done.'

'We're going for a tipple, me and Marco.'

'Or would you rather we stayed?' Marco asks.

'Gosh, no.'

'MUMMY?' SHE IS whispering.

Roxy is tired; she doesn't say anything, her eyes stay closed. Louise is standing next to the bed. Roxy has told her not to shout so loudly in the morning. She is only allowed out of bed when it is light and then she can come and lie down next to her quietly, as long as she doesn't wake her up.

'Mummy?' Louise carefully gets into the bed. She shunts up close to her but doesn't quite touch her. Roxy feels her daughter's breath. Her eyelids are heavy; she is still in the night but she knows that Louise is waiting for a sign of life.

Roxy can't help smiling right through her tiredness— that wide-awake face, almost stuck to hers. She cautiously opens her eyes. Louise laughs immediately. Roxy's waking up is good news for somebody. Roxy pinches her daughter's side and Louise lets out a rippling laugh. She bites her daughter's nose, Louise screeches and licks her mother's cheek. Roxy buries her head deep under the dirty bedclothes that have not been changed for ages. Too much has been eaten in the bed, too many dreams, too much sweat. Louise copies and finds her mother. Licking each other's cheeks, pinching, screeching and snorting under the bedclothes. They are a pair of animals in their filthy sty.

Roxy would be happy now if she wasn't aware of the fact that Arthur can't see how happy she is and she hasn't got anyone else who might be interested. This is the lot.

She rubs her face in her daughter's hair, inhales her smell: sweet, salty, everything; feeling, knowing that Louise is everything and that if anything happened to her daughter she would die too. It isn't an anxious thought but a lucid observation she makes every morning now. And then she gets up.

On the stairs she smells fried eggs. Her mother is standing at the stove.

'A fry-up,' her father says.

'Croque madame,' her mother says.

'You'll be meaning a fried-egg sandwich.'

'Do we have to do this?'

'Good morning,' Roxy says.

'Good morning, doll. Pretty unexpected, huh?'

Her mother never normally gets out of bed.

'Yeah,' Roxy says, and then adds, 'Great, though.'

'What's great?' Louise asks.

'That Grandma got up early.' Louise crawls under the table.

'Give me your plate.' The table has been laid. Although Roxy doesn't like big breakfasts, she passes her plate like a mother forced to eat the biscuits her child has baked. The dog comes into the kitchen and sniffs at Louise under the table.

'Stinky dog,' Louise says, crawling away and clamping herself to Roxy's leg.

'Your father has made coffee.'

'I don't know how that coffee machine works,' he says. 'I used that little one, but you can squeeze three cups out of it.'

'I don't have any filters.'

'Bog roll's all right for that.'

Smoke is coming from the little percolator. The toilet paper is perfumed and now Roxy gets the strange mixture of smells in the kitchen: fried eggs, dog, coffee, and perfumed toilet paper. She lifts up Louise, hides her face in her hair and tries to smell only her daughter. Then she lifts the child up high above her head.

'I'm flying,' Louise says.

'You're as light as a feather,' Roxy says, letting her daughter sink and stretching her arms up again, up and down, up and down, taking giant strides through the kitchen, proving to her daughter that she is strong. She puts Louise on the kitchen table, panting.

Her father says, 'Hey you little stinker, want to come for a ride in Grandad's truck?'

'We're about to have breakfast,' her mother says.

'Or are we going in the truck?'

'Truck,' Louise says.

He picks up the child, lifts her onto his shoulders and leaves.

'What a rude bugger he is,' her mother says.

Roxy says, 'She's not clingy.'

'She's an easy child.'

They sit down.

'Do you want to talk about it?'

Roxy doesn't speak.

'Rather not, then?'

'Oh, I do want to.'

Without the pressure of having Louise around her, she feels how early it is and how tired she is.

Her mother says, 'And your life was all so perfect.'

'I think I want to go and lie down.'

'Then go and have a lie down, dear.'

Before she's got back upstairs she's already being troubled by the words: 'I want to die.' It's not good for a child to have a mother who is so frequently troubled by a line like that. Once in bed, she wonders how to save her child from herself. Really, you should gradually transfer a child into someone else's arms—a better person. But Roxy wants to keep her child and she understands the parents who take their own lives and those of their children at the same time.

The five-toned klaxon of her father's Scania echoes through the street. Louise must be loving it.

If Roxy stays upstairs for long enough, she won't have to see her mother again until she's drunk. It's easier to handle like that than gradually watching it happen.

She is awoken by footsteps. It's Jane, who wasn't supposed to come until the afternoon.

'What time is it?'

'Half past one. Had a good nap?'

Jane sits down on the chair she'd sat in when Roxy was getting dressed for the funeral. The curtains are closed but the sun is shining through them.

'Louise?'

'She's off somewhere with your dad.'

'Still? And Mum?'

'Watching TV.'

'Is she very drunk?'

'Yes.'

'Okay.'

'*Okay?*'

Roxy sits up. 'You mustn't say anything about it.'

'Why not?'

'Then she starts crying, and she really isn't any trouble when she's drunk.'

'Is it a problem if she starts crying?'

'Please don't. Arthur couldn't stop himself.'

'From making your mother cry?'

'He did it for me, he'd say. He couldn't bear seeing her like that and he'd start to lecture her. She'd cry. I'd hide away somewhere so as not to hear it. By the end, she'd be hysterical and he'd be angry with me. Atrocious. Impossible—the pair of them. Please, leave her alone.'

'I'm not doing anything.'

'And later, he said he did it for Louise.'

'Does Louise like to visit them?'

'Hasn't been much. In the summer it's all right: then you can go outside. The neighbours have got sheep. She likes that.'

'Are you getting up?'

'Your hair is shorter.'

Jane feels at her head. 'Much too short.'

'I like it like that.'

'Are you getting up? Otherwise you won't be able to sleep tonight.'

The word 'night' unsettles Roxy immediately. 'I'm frightened.'

'Give it time.'

'I don't know if things are going to be all right.'

Jane is already standing up.

'I've often wanted to die,' Roxy says. 'Arthur must have

told you. It's not a problem; it's a bit annoying, like a fly, a bothersome sound. It only gets difficult when the fly buzzes around your head all day.'

'No, Arthur never said.'

'He didn't?'

'No.'

'Really?'

'No.'

Jane waits.

'Half one already?' Roxy says.

'Marco's here.'

Marco is sitting on a bar stool, exactly as Roxy had once imagined, but people have only started coming in so casually since Arthur's death. The two police officers opened the door that night and it has never closed.

'How are things now?' Marco asks.

Her mother is lying on the sofa asleep, the TV still on, the dog at her feet. Roxy closes the interconnecting doors.

'I don't feel like talking.'

'Do you want me to go?'

'No, you talk.'

'What do you want to know?'

'Something nice.'

'Something nice?'

'Yes please.'

Marco doesn't say anything.

'Do you know any jokes?' Roxy asks.

'Do you like jokes?'

'No, I was just wondering whether you knew any.'

'Jokes aren't really my thing.'

'Do you know the one about the bear and the hunter?'

'Everyone knows that!'

'No they don't.'

'That's so old,' he says, twirling his wrist in the air.

'Seriously, does everyone know that joke? Jane?'

'Well little man,' Marco says in a deep voice, 'are you going to give me that blow job or not?'

Roxy has to laugh hard at the delicate man on the bar stool, legs crossed, imitating the horny bear. For a moment she has escaped.

'Yes,' she says, 'that was nice,' immediately feeling an ache in her stomach after the brief flight, pain that must have been there for days but which she only feels now after its temporary cessation. Her face contorts.

'What?'

She says, 'I can't do it.'

'I know,' he says. 'It's a lot to accept.'

'*Accept?*' she repeats too loudly, as though he'd asked permission to beat her up.

The doorbell rings and Jane is already on her feet.

Louise runs in ahead of her grandfather. The dog barks; Roxy's mother moves.

'Where have you two been all of this time?'

'We had some food in Breda.'

'At Aunty Frieda's,' Louise says.

'You don't have an Aunty Frieda.'

'Kids!' her father says. 'I'm just popping over to The Pump.'

'You're going again? Right now?'

'They're waiting for me.' He's already gone.

'Shame,' Marco says.

'Yes,' Roxy says. 'He has no trouble making friends.'

When she can't sleep during the night and hears noises downstairs, she gets out of bed. Her father has come home.

There's a fat stranger on the sofa.

He holds up a hand. 'Hi.'

'Hello.'

'Roxy?' Her father calls her from the basement.

'Yes?'

'That's Wim!'

'Hello,' Roxy says again.

'Hi. You're Roxy.'

'Yes.'

'I'm Wim.'

'Hi.'

'Were you already asleep?'

'Yes.'

'Did we wake you up?'

'No, don't worry. I slept too much during the day.'

'Not a good idea.'

'No.'

Her father has fetched a bottle of wine. 'They had to close; we're having another drink. Is the wine in the basement still all right?'

'Yes, you have to take the ones from the top.'

'Joining us?'

'Louise wakes up very early.'

'Oh yes, are you off tomorrow?'

'Off?'

'Are you off on holiday?'

'No—what do you mean?'

'That's what she said in the truck: "We're going on holiday tomorrow. A really long drive." I thought, she can't really mean tomorrow.'

'We're not going on holiday at all. She must mean that we went on holiday,' Roxy says. 'We drove a long time when we did.'

'No, she said, "We're going on holiday."'

'Yeah, well, she also says she can see Smurfs.'

'That's a good 'un,' Wim says.

Her father opens the kitchen cupboards looking for a corkscrew.

'Bottom left,' Roxy says.

'Sure you don't want a drink?'

'No, I'm going back to bed.'

'Sleep tight, love.'

'Night night,' Wim says.

Roxy realizes that Louise wants to go on holiday. It's not a misunderstanding.

Louise sleeps on her back, her arms stretched out above her. She is still in the high-sided cot but has long been able to climb out herself. Roxy kneels beside the bed, leans against the balusters, and looks at Louise. Her child, too, knows that acceptance isn't an option. They have to escape.

A month before Arthur's death, the three of them went to Vienna. It was Roxy's idea—it was about time she got the urge to go somewhere.

Arthur's desires were both concrete and wide-ranging. He wanted to go to Vietnam in the winter, travel through Russia by train. He wanted a second home in the Eifel region, to live in Finland again at some point, spend Christmas in Morocco, get bespoke shoes, sell his company, and set up his own magazine. In contrast to his wishes, Roxy's paled: they were diverse, slow, latent. It wasn't nice to be the only one who wanted something; it made him feel lonely. And that's why this year, Roxy had said she really wanted to go to Vienna, blurting out something about pastries and Viennese coffee houses.

She had been seventeen when Arthur took her to the Pompadour tearoom in Amsterdam. Their second date. The pies Roxy was used to were made of pre-packed bases from the supermarket. Her mother would throw a tin of cherries in syrup over them. The whipped cream was the only thing she'd make. She didn't like squirty cream—that rubbish wasn't entering *their* house. That was what her mother was like—turning her nose up at quite random things. She had to vent her snobbery on something, however mindless and misplaced that snobbery might be.

In Pompadour, Roxy realized she would have been better off not mentioning the pre-packed bases she'd liked so much as a child. A rare, happy childhood memory was ruined in one fell blow. She could no longer go back to her mother's pies once she'd tried the minuscule chocolate truffle tarts in Pompadour, wiping the last few crumbs from her plate with her finger and eating them.

Arthur said, 'If you like tart, you should go to Vienna,' barely realizing that Roxy had just been on a world tour. He forgot saying it, but Roxy remembered, like she'd once remembered that she should marry a doctor. She saved these concrete goals: they were signposts in the peculiar world of desires. So when, as usual, Arthur brought up the subject of holidays and she saw him looking at his wife and her inability to desire with obvious chagrin, it was time to bring up Vienna.

'I'd love to go to Vienna at some point.' It worked; it cheered him up. Roxy fed him his own ideas, acted as though they were hers and provided him with momentary respite from his loneliness. Of course it was a crazy plan to go and eat patisserie in Vienna for three weeks with a toddler in tow, but these were the exact kinds of plans that had made them the happiest in the early days of their relationship. Whether that had meant a week in Paris without leaving their hotel room and thus seeing nothing of Paris, or flying to Morocco for four days. They were in love.

The exhausting Viennese patisserie quest had seemed like a good plan, but turned into an unpleasant memory. For the first time in a long while, Roxy paid attention to their expenditure. She saw Louise's half-eaten tarts and wondered how many cake bases you could buy for the price of that half-piece of tart. Of course, there were moments when everything was fine, like the sunny days during a wet summer, and she still believed back then that the exception was the real truth. But what her daughter was longing for now, and Roxy understood this, was not that holiday but their journey back home. They had been planning to take two days over it and on the way they'd stay in a hotel, but they were fed up with hotels. They were fed up with holidays; they wanted to go home.

'Let's drive on further,' Roxy had said. With stop-offs, it was perfectly possible to do it in a day and a night. Arthur agreed. It was absurd to drive twelve hundred kilometres in one go but because they both wanted to, he had managed to pull it off.

Louise was singing and chattering on the backseat as the sun climbed higher and it grew hotter and busier on the roads. The schnitzels in the roadside restaurants, the pizza slices, muffins, and chocolate doughnuts tasted better than the patisserie in Hotel Sacher. They saw the sun sink down again; the colours of the sky changed by the hour, the roads emptied, Louise carried on singing and chatting. 'Look: a forest; look: a truck; look: a cow; look: a horse ...' And when she finally fell asleep after midnight, Arthur and Roxy had to talk, sing, and play guessing games to keep whoever was driving awake, just as Roxy had sung to her father in the truck when she was thirteen. She'd sing all the songs she knew for him: children's songs, English songs—half of them phonetically, her father didn't understand anyway. An international trucker and he didn't speak any other language than Dutch; he got away with it. She sang everything by Harry Belafonte, her mother's hero.

When her father threatened to doze off, she'd cry, 'Day-o, day-ay-ay-o. Daylight come and he wan' go home.'

But sometimes she was tired herself and he would poke her awake: 'Sing, Roxy.'

THE UNDERTAKER, MARCEL Hendriks, has arrived. It's hot and she's only wearing a T-shirt. She was expecting Jane when she went to the door.

'Is it a bad time?'

He glances at her breasts briefly, she notices, he notices her noticing and Roxy sees the escape route.

'No,' she says, 'it's not a bad time at all. Come in.' She follows him barefoot into the kitchen. It would be normal to put a dressing gown on now, or a pair of jogging pants, something more than this.

'We always make a follow-up phone call, but I happened to be in the neighbourhood.'

'How nice,' she says. 'Nice of you to drop in.' It sounds stupid but she has to let him know that it's all right, that she fully agrees with what has now become inevitable. The unknown man has suddenly become a body. Unthinkable that she hadn't noticed the spot where his shirt pinches his upper arms before.

'Are you reasonably happy with the way everything went?'

He's teasing her.

'I have no complaints.'

The whole dialogue comes across to her as a pointless porn film script.

She says languorously, 'I've never looked at so many different coffin handles before in my life,' and it's the horniest line she's ever spoken.

To her amazement, the conversation continues this way for a while. Marcel even gets a questionnaire out of his bag.

'I'll come and pick it up later.' He seems to want to leave.

'I'd like to thank you,' Roxy says. She puts her arms around him; he allows it. She has to stand on tiptoes. 'You're tall.' He smells of wood and sweat. There are bumping noises upstairs and he frees himself.

'Your daughter?'

'My parents.'

'Sorry, this isn't possible.'

'Are you coming back tomorrow?'

'Tomorrow?'

'I'll have filled it in by then.' She giggles.

'It's not particularly urgent.'

'It's Arthur's day tomorrow.'

'Arthur's day?'

'I mean ... the babysitter picks up Louise.'

'Sorry.'

'What for?'

'I'll be in touch, ma'am.'

Ma'am. That's ridiculous, he's taking this childish game too far. He turns away from her. What does he want? She can hardly drag him back. He's already left.

Roxy looks at the kitchen dresser, just the right height to hit her head on. She carefully rests her head against it and pushes hard into the wood, consciously, slowly increasing the pressure. She thought she knew what shame was, but it can always get worse, she sees. Then she realizes she hasn't heard the door close yet. He's still in the hallway, unsure. He can still come back. Roxy counts. When she gets to forty-three, Marcel opens the door very gently and leaves. Almost a minute. She's no fool: it's still possible.

In the afternoon, the pot roast is on the stove. Her mother, originally from Limburg, has insisted on cooking. She is peeling potatoes. Her father is crawling through the kitchen with Louise on his back.

Marcel needed three hours to think about it, then she got a message on her mobile: 'Hi Roxy, would it be all right if I picked up the questionnaire at around eleven tomorrow morning? Marcel.' Just his first name. Transparent.

She texted back, 'See you tomorrow. R.'

'Mum,' she says, 'it smells delicious.'

'You're joking,' her father says.

'Yes, you'll have to go back home either tonight or early tomorrow morning. I'll manage.'

They say nothing. That was too fast, of course.

'I really appreciate it,' she says, 'but ...'

'We don't mind staying, honey,' her mother says.

Her father pauses, still on all fours. 'Would you rather we went? Are we getting in the way?'

'Maybe you ... can take Louise to ... the Efteling theme park tomorrow.'

'That's quite a long way away,' her mother says.

'Louise, darling,' Roxy says, 'do you want to go to the Fairy Tale Forest?'

'I want to go to Smurf Land,' Louise says.

'That doesn't exist.'

'Is the dog allowed in Efteling?'

'Jesus,' her father says. 'What do you think?'

That evening, she washes herself for the first time in a week. The undertaker is married and has three children, all girls. He showed Louise the pictures. There was a time when Roxy had a view about messing with other women's husbands. Now, in practice, it becomes a minor detail, something like him working on Thursdays but not on Fridays. It's the excitement that counts and she grabs it with both hands, the only rope that can pull her out of the swamp.

ROXY HAS PUT on her high heels so that she can kiss him right away. They stand in the hallway with their mouths open, almost motionless against each other, sharing breath. Then he encircles her face with both his hands and his tongue finds hers. Her own arms do nothing, all the tension flows out through them and she feels herself slipping away like a fish: slender, smooth, wet, slippery.

She takes him to the large sofa; they don't speak. He doesn't let her undress him, he does that himself, quickly, but his hands are never away from her for long. She undresses herself too, it seems there's no time. She holds his cock, tastes him. He uses his fingers to feel how wet she is and kisses her down there, licks, tastes—when their mouths come back together they taste each other and themselves in their saliva and wetness. His cock pushes.

'May I?'

'Just for a moment then.'

He enters her and licks her lips, just as he did down below. She knows him now; they have a common history and she understands that Arthur wasn't able to do without this. She loves him again.

He pulls out of her in time and ejaculates on her stomach. She doesn't stay lying there for long. When you've finally been kissed awake, you don't just lie there at your leisure, looking around. She pushes him off her, smiling, wipes herself with her T-shirt, jumps to her feet and throws him his clothes.

'Are we going to make a habit of this?' he asks.

'Back to work, you,' she says. 'Dead people are waiting.'

For the first time since Arthur's death, she goes upstairs to her study, looks at the books she has written and wonders whether everything really has to be revised. She opens her second novel: it's about a man with a passion for collecting. *One Man And His House.* Her editor had already expressed his doubts about that one.

'It's rather ... different,' she can still hear him say. They bloody published it, it can't be all bad.

In her last book, she'd had a woman do the opposite—every day she threw something away. Lots of contemplation next to a dumpster. Arthur had given the book to their mechanic without asking her.

'Cool, right? He wanted to read something you'd written.'

'That book,' the man had said after their last major service, 'you'll have to explain it to me, love.' She'd stuttered; she'd said, 'It is a strange novel,' and it had felt as though she was dirtying herself.

She curses again. If everything she can't explain is worthless, that doesn't leave much. Perhaps there isn't much left. She slams the book shut; she doesn't have time.

She can catch up on those years; it's possible now that

she's awake. She has been practising, that's the thing. Other people study for years to no avail, she did this, that was her excuse. Excuse for what? Not living? That's not possible. Sleeping for ten years is crazy; it can't possibly be right.

Her parents return from Efteling shattered. Her father is red-faced from the sun and his irritation. Roxy lifts up Louise, her cheeks are sticky. She kisses her and tastes chocolate milkshake and ice cream.

Her mother hangs around on the doorstep and tries to remain aloof; she always does that when she's drunk.

Roxy dances with her child in her arms and sings, 'Day-o, day-ay-ay-o. Tell me all the things you saw, sweetheart.'

'Don't know.'

'Daddy! Day-o, day-o.'

'Sure,' her father says.

Roxy walks up to her mother, wraps an arm around her and tries to dance around with her, her daughter still on her hip.

Her mother staggers. 'Not right now.'

'Was it fun, Mum?'

'It's got really commercial.'

'Have you been before, then?'

'It's very noisy there,' her father says.

'Dad, did we ever go to Efteling?'

'Are you complaining?'

'Louise, darling, did you see the red shoes from the fairy tale?'

'I want to watch TV.'

The dog barks in the garden. The doors are shut. He stands with his front paws against the glass.

'That poor creature,' her mother says, letting him in.

The dog jumps up against her, she clings to the doorpost and then he runs enthusiastically around the kitchen table. Roxy hasn't seen the dog this active all week. His claws make scratching noises on the smooth flooring; he shoots between her father's legs and the man topples over. It's not entirely clear how it happens, but all of a sudden he's sitting on the floor.

'Bloody hell.'

'Bloody hell,' Louise says.

'Ouch, are you all right?'

He gets up, groaning. His knees creak.

'What happened there?' Roxy asks.

She expects him to swear at the dog, but he says, 'It's too bloody slippery, that marble. Does that Filipino of yours rub green soap into it or what?'

'Can I have choco-milk?' Louise asks.

'Got to pop out.'

'Are you going to eat at home?' Roxy calls after him.

'I'll get a burger in The Pump.'

The front door slams shut.

'Day-o, day-ay-ay-o. Daylight come and he wan' go home,' Roxy sings with her daughter on her hip.

'Don't sing, Mummy.'

Liza arrives right after Jane, as though she's waited for her to arrive first. Roxy has put the plastic trays from the Surinamese takeaway in the microwave. Yesterday's leftovers are on the stove.

'We're having pot roast with flatbread.'

'Where is everyone?' Liza asks.

'Louise is under that blanket,' she points to the sofa where the child has fallen asleep, 'Mum is in bed and Dad's in the pub.' She can't stop smiling.

'What's happened?' Liza asks.

Roxy wants to make her story exciting. She searches for words, but then says, 'I got laid.'

'By who?'

'Marcel.'

'Who's Marcel?' Liza asks.

'Marcel Hendriks.'

'Who's Marcel Hendriks?'

'Hendriks' Funeral Services. For an immaculate and befitting funeral.'

'My word,' Jane says, but she's laughing.

'I fucked the undertaker.'

'You're kidding me.'

'You're smiling, Jane, you're smiling!'

'Too right.'

Liza screams like a teenager, 'You go, girl!'

Jane shakes her head in mock indignation. 'Was it good?'

'Wonderful.'

'Good for you.'

Jane's approval makes Roxy's happiness complete.

Louise wakes up and says, 'My dad is called Arthur.'

IT'S STILL COLD in the kitchen. Roxy and Louise are alone. Her mother's breakfast attempts have run aground. She can be certain that her mother, a creature of habit, won't get up before midday now, and that her father, who is used to getting up ridiculously early, will pick up his old routine again and will have found a café somewhere in the city centre.

Roxy is looking for bread. There's no bread. The others have done the shopping up to now. They eat the last biscuits and find half a packet of prawn crackers left over from yesterday's takeaway.

There's a pile of paperwork lying ready on the kitchen table, Arthur's admin, their admin, which she is still going through with Jane. She has looked through everything, in as much as she can understand what it's about, and there are Post-its stuck to pages, mainly with questions that begin: In the worst case scenario, does this mean that ...?

Louise wants to watch TV and Roxy says, 'All right, just this once,' but she's been saying that for a few days now and she thinks about sitting in front of the television with her mother watching *Lingo* and her mother saying, '*Lingo* is educational, you'll learn something useful.' She believed that back then. Later, she believed, in any case, that her mother had believed it and now she realizes that her mother had said it out loud to reassure herself, to justify her habits.

Instead of staying silent, Roxy repeats it, only louder, 'Just this once then,' and when Jane comes in and says, 'Are you watching TV again?' Louise says, 'Just this once then.'

Jane pulls the pile of papers toward her.

'Do you like having your parents here?'

'Is that a serious question?'

'What do you mean?'

'Of course I don't like having them here.'

'So why don't you ask them to leave?'

'They'll leave on their own, they won't be able to hold out for long.'

'Why don't you send them away?'

'Bloody hell, you're just like Arthur. If you don't do exactly what you want to, you're a hypocrite and dishonest and weak. What kind of a simple world do you two come from?'

'It was only a question.'

'Sorry.'

'I presume that outburst was intended for Arthur and not me.'

'Arthur wasn't keen on my parents.'

'And you are?'

Roxy picks up the funeral papers. 'Maybe I can get Hendriks to give me a discount.'

'I miss him,' Jane says.

Roxy almost asks who.

'I miss him,' she rubs her eyes. 'Sorry.'

'You don't have to apologize for that,' Roxy says, as she feels a stabbing pain—love for Arthur is an attack on her. Again Jane rubs her eyes. Don't cry, Roxy thinks. Please don't cry.

'I don't know who else I can talk to about it. My girl-friend is busy with her PhD thesis and she can't handle this on top, so I can't bother her.' She stops rubbing and lets the tears run down her cheeks. This has to stop immediately. Roxy has to find the right words and offer the right support. She can't lose Jane.

'I miss him.'

Roxy sits next to her. 'We're going out,' she moves the papers aside. 'We'll do this another time. We're going out,' she says again, like a person with a plan.

'But I still have to explain those insurance packages and we have to change the mortgage and file the final return ...'

'What the hell's that?'

'Jesus, don't you know anything, Roxy? The final re-turn! I have to explain *everything* to you, everything!'

'Oh, the tax return? Of course I know what a tax return is, woman, everyone knows what a tax return is. Fuck the tax return, we're going out. The fair's in town for fuck's sake and we haven't even been yet.'

Jane laughs and cries, 'I hate funfairs.'

'Do you like candy floss?'

'Yeah, that's okay.'

'Come on then. Louise, shoes on!'

There's an old-fashioned wooden caterpillar, the only attraction all three of them can go on. Louise sits on Roxy's lap, they slither across the smooth bench toward

Jane at the first turn, a tangle of people, Louise giggles and all three of them scream when the roof closes down over them. The innocence of their pleasure moves Roxy. Tears threaten but she is able to hold them back.

Roxy buys three sticks of candy floss, the largest size. Jane has to be happy, she has to be strong; they need her. Text messages from Marcel. He can come early tomorrow. It's not Arthur's day but Louise can watch television, her mother never gets out of bed. It'll have to do because this pleasure can't be allowed to stop.

Roxy eats not only her own candy floss but also her daughter's and part of Jane's, despite feeling sick. Roxy loves candy floss. Some things have to stay the same. She is walking around the fair with Arthur's PA, whom she used to be afraid of, and lusts after her husband's undertaker, but she still loves candy floss.

LOUISE IS SITTING in her bedroom watching a Smurfs DVD on the laptop. Roxy is fucking the undertaker on the sofa. She quickly gets dressed again when it's over, but Marcel takes his time and then sits back down on the sofa. He picks up a supermarket flyer that was lying on the coffee table.

'What are you doing?' Roxy asks.

'What?'

'What are you doing?'

'I'm looking at the special offers.'

He looks bigger when he's sitting. She coughs. Louise comes in.

'Hey Titch,' Marcel says.

'I'm thirsty.'

'I'll see Marcel out and then I'll make you some juice.'

Marcel kisses her neck, sucks her ear.

Louise says, 'He's biting your ear.'

Roxy takes a step back, her hand on Marcel's cheek, a strong, badly-shaven jaw. It resembles a maternal gesture, then she goes over to Louise and doesn't think to brush the child's cheek, she squats and presses her cheek to her daughter's.

'I'm thirsty.'

'Just a sec.'

She opens the door for Marcel and kisses him on the doorstep. His hands have just disappeared under her t-shirt when a man on the other side of the street takes a photograph.

'Oops,' Roxy says. 'We've been caught on film.' So people *are* watching her. Marcel snorts and smiles nervously. Then her father comes walking up, whistling. He looks from them to the photographer and back again, quickly weighing up the situation. He waves at the photographer and winks.

'My dad.'

Her father draws a punch, hitting Marcel's upper arm. 'Keep on smiling, mate,' before slipping indoors.

Marcel tries to reach his car as calmly as possible but in his attempts to appear nonchalant, he comes across as wooden. He gets into his car with its company logo and the photograph snaps again. That was a bit dumb, Roxy thinks. Louise calls her.

'That was Marcel.'

'Yes,' her father says, 'and Marcel will be in the paper tomorrow.'

'Yeah, we weren't thinking.'

'He's an adult.'

'Right,' Roxy affirms, briefly considering feeling responsible, but that's not a feeling that suits her. She easily shakes it off.

Three days later, they look at the newspapers in the supermarket. Louise is allowed to pick a magazine. She pulls a *Donald Duck* off the shelf, while Roxy peruses the tabloids. She finds a small photo on page fourteen and is happy. It's a dubious pleasure but now that pleasure has become such a rare, welcome thing, she ignores her doubts. She buys the magazine along with too many *Donald Ducks* and some car magazines for her father so that her purchase won't stand out.

Jane is already inside; they'll finally straighten out the mass of paperwork this afternoon. Liza is there too, she's sitting next to Roxy's mother in the kitchen. This is her mother's best time, early afternoon. Her father is searching for the football scores on Teletext in the living room.

'I spotted Jane's car,' Liza says, 'and I'm out of coffee.'

'Do you need to borrow some coffee?'

'No, of course not,' Jane says. 'She'll have coffee here.'

'Your coffee's better.'

'Do you mean my coffee or Arthur's coffee?'

Jane says, 'No one likes your coffee, darl'. Liza wants an espresso. Come here, I'll teach you.'

Her father has been listening in. 'I can't taste the difference.'

'That doesn't say much,' her mother says.

Jane demonstrates how you use the machine and Liza stands close to her. She reminds Roxy of her own daughter, so easily leaning toward strangers in shops and trams.

'Now me,' Liza says.

Once her parents have left, Roxy will be the only adult in the house who can't use the coffee machine. She has to learn before Louise does; there's time enough.

She throws the newspaper onto the kitchen table. 'I'm in it.'

Her father picks it up. '"Rombouts widow seeks comfort in arms of undertaker." The rats!'

'Give it here,' her mother says. She looks and says, 'When did you do that then?'

'Undertaker,' her father says, 'well, well.'

'Is it on the front page too?' her mother asks.

'Jesus,' Roxy says, 'of course not. We look quite good, don't we?'

'It's a small picture.'

Her mother passes the paper to Liza, who was already reading it over her shoulder.

Roxy wants to laugh: pleasure. 'Something for your scrapbook, Mum.'

'Marcel's married,' Jane says.

'Is that my responsibility?'

'Bit shitty for his wife,' she says.

'Yes,' Roxy says, but she doesn't feel it. 'These things happen,' and she's amazed at her lack of compassion. She should understand what it's like for his wife. She was the one who couldn't read a paper without crying before, who'd lie awake thinking she'd insulted the neighbour by not waving. Now she has been transformed into a wonderful icy fish, freed of empathy, and she says, 'All's fair in love and war.'

'Love?' Liza asks.

Jane shakes as she uses the espresso machine.

'You drink too much coffee,' Roxy says. 'You're shaking.'

'Ready,' Louise says, coming into the kitchen, her small cardboard suitcase suddenly bursting open. All her Smurfs pyjamas fall onto the floor.

'And where are you going?' Liza asks.

'Holiday.'

'Oh?'

'We're going on holiday,' Louise says again.

'Oh yeah?' Roxy says.

'Where's Daddy?' She regularly asks this question to which everyone still patiently and calmly replies that he's dead, at which point Louise sometimes cries for a while and sometimes she just carries on with whatever she's doing, but it comes out now so routinely that Roxy says, 'Where do you think?'

Louise's face crumples. Roxy regrets it immediately.

Louise answers quietly, 'Daddy is dead.'

She shouldn't have made her daughter say it. Even if she knew the answer, she was asking for a reason: someone else had to say it, not her.

Louise doesn't cry. She sighs like an adult reluctantly accepting something, which only makes it worse. Roxy doesn't want to see her daughter like this. She squats down in front of her. She is wearing the high heels that Marcel likes, maybe he thinks she only wears them for him, but the high heels make squatting easier and she can be perfectly eye-to-eye with Louise, see what she sees. Roxy picks up the pyjamas and puts them in the case.

'We're going on holiday,' Louise says, but without conviction. 'Aren't we?' she adds and now all Roxy has to do is say no.

'Yes,' Roxy says, since she's the one who can make this possible.

'Yes?'

'Yes, we're going on holiday.'

'Now?'

'Well ... tomorrow would be easier.'

Disbelief creeps back into her daughter's expression and Roxy hurriedly says, 'No, now, of course, yes, now.'

Her daughter smiles, it's so easy to make her smile. 'Now?'

'Of course.'

The child believes her. She can make anything come true.

'Oh,' Jane says, 'that's nice—so shall I just finish off your admin for you then?' She slaps the pile of paperwork.

'You can come with us,' Louise says.

'Yes,' Roxy says, meaning it. 'You can come with us.'

'You're the boss,' Jane says. 'I do need a holiday—my girlfriend is no use to me right now.'

'Really?' Roxy asks as though she, in turn, can't believe that mummy's coming too. She tries not to look at her real mother.

'Seriously, my girlfriend will be pleased I'm not around to bother her.'

'And me?' Liza says.

They look at her in surprise.

'I want to come too.'

'Of course you're coming with us,' Roxy says. For the first time all four of them laugh together: Roxy, Jane and Liza, and even Louise—none of them quite realizing why, but all of them just as hard and just as long, because Louise is three and likes to join in, the way birds fly in formation. There's never one bird who gets the urge to be different and tries to go the other way.

'Grandad and Grandma not come,' Louise points at them.

'What did you say, sweetie?' Roxy's mother asks.

'Where are we going?' Jane asks.

'To the seaside,' Roxy says quickly because they have to keep the momentum going, impulsiveness doesn't go with uncertainty and deliberation.

'The seaside?' Jane says, 'That's not a holiday, that's a day out.'

'Mediterranean coast.'

'The Mediterranean, naturally.'

Her father sings, 'The Med Sea, as blue as can be.'

'Grandad not coming.'

'You're frightening the child with all that caterwauling,' her mother says.

'You two can stay here another night if you like,' Roxy says, 'you can close up the house tomorrow, right?'

As they pack, her mother lies with a bottle of wine and the dog on the sofa in front of the television. It's almost cosy, two pets in the house.

Roxy has paid for everything since they've been staying with her. She doesn't know how bad their debts are. They don't respond to any of her prying; they won't tell her.

'Dad,' she says, 'could you pop out for some fags for me?' and she gives him two two-hundred euro notes from Arthur's black cashbox. 'And get a couple of cartons for Mum while you're at it.'

'Don't be such a bossy boots,' he says.

'And never mind about the change—birthday present.'

Her father accepts the money. 'Flash, aren't we?'

Appointments have to be cancelled. Jane has an important meeting with a distributor who used to work with Arthur. She goes into the conservatory.

Louise is singing as she makes piles of chocolate spread sandwiches. They catch Jane's words from the conservatory.

'Arthur's wife ... no, not great ... needs to take a break ... Terrible ... Only three, yes ... poor child.'

Louise is still singing. Liza takes the jar of Liquorice Allsorts out of the cupboard and feeds them to Louise until she's quiet.

'Great ... thank you,' they hear Jane say. 'Yes, I need to look after her ... thank you ... I appreciate that.'

Jane looks at her telephone a few times to check the connection has actually been cut off and then shouts, 'Holiday!'

After that, Liza has to go into the conservatory to cancel going to her parents' wedding anniversary and a weekend on Texel island with the whole family.

'Can you really get out of it?' Roxy asks.

'It's no problem,' Liza says earnestly. *That does seem quite important*, Roxy thinks, almost forgetting that someone has actually died.

They hear, 'Arthur and Roxy's daughter ... She's not doing so well ... really clingy with me now ... photographers? ... Yes, a lot of paparazzi ... awful ... asked whether I could go ...'

Then Liza begins to cry with deep sobs, 'She's so small ... keeps asking, "Where's Daddy?" and I ...'

Roxy and Jane are so taken aback that they don't do anything other than stare at the sobbing Liza in the conservatory. Even Louise, who stops chewing, looks at the dramatic scene behind glass, her liquorice-filled mouth falling open. It's a while before Roxy and Jane avert their gaze and begin to potter around the kitchen. Then it's quiet.

'Liza!' Louise cries. She looks into the conservatory. Liza is beaming; she opens the door.

'Right,' she says, 'that's sorted.' She doesn't look shaken

at all, there's no trace of sadness on her face. They're impressed, proud of her.

The front door stays open that afternoon, the mat wedged to keep it open. Liza goes backward and forward to her student digs to fetch things. Roxy parks the suv on the pavement so that they can fill it easily. Jane takes her car home and gets a taxi back. She has a large suitcase; she's taking the holiday seriously.

From time to time they remember other appointments and go into the conservatory to cancel dentists, doctors, friends, and family in hushed, sorrowful tones. They mustn't be cancelling things because it's fun to do so. They must cancel them only because there's no alternative, because the misery stops you from thinking and talking, because, depressed, you fill the car with only what's strictly necessary. No one has to know that they are chucking inflatable animals into the suv's boot, singing, and filling the glove compartment with liquorice and cigarettes.

The car doors are open; no space for pedestrians along the pavement.

Roxy's father comes outside with her phone. She doesn't pick up.

'Who is it?'

'Marcel Hendriks.'

'Really?'

'Have you spoken to him,' Jane asks, 'since that photo?'

'Leave it,' Roxy says. She crawls into the back of the car to stack up the cases properly.

'A message,' her father calls. 'Shall I read it?'

'What's he say?'

'Call me. I'm up shit creek.'

Roxy gets out of the car. 'Rubbish.'

'No, really.'

'Did he really write that?'

She takes the phone.

'How funny.'

'I don't get it,' Liza says. 'What's funny?'

'What he said,' Roxy says. '"Up shit creek", that's something my dad would say. It's just like him.'

Her mother comes outside now with a large, drunken smile on her face.

'Funny yes,' Liza says. 'Shit creek.'

'There's a real Shit Creek in America somewhere,' Roxy's mother says.

'How did you know that?' Liza asks.

'Shouldn't you give him a quick call?' Jane suggests.

'I can't call,' Roxy says. 'I'm on holiday.'

AS HER PARENTS wave them off, it's easy to love them. Roxy drives; she toots another couple of times. They turn the corner and quietness descends.

On the ring road, Roxy says, 'That was them doing their best. Can you imagine?'

Jane gets the liquorice out of the glove box.

'You didn't go to university at all?' Liza asks.

'I studied *Countdown*.'

'*Countdown?*'

'At least ten years, every night: *Countdown*. Seven, eight, nine letters—I can beat anyone.'

'Rubbish.'

'No, really.'

'I don't believe you. Jane, do you believe her?'

'Yes,' Jane says, 'I read about it.'

'In my book?'

'Yes.'

Roxy blushes because she'd quoted herself word-for-word, a witty answer she pulled out of her sleeve for familiar questions. Her alter ego in her first novel had it down pat.

'Why did you watch *Countdown* every day?' Liza asks.

Roxy searches for new words, but her youth has become a novel she repeats out loud.

'Because we had dinner like that, in bed, my mum and me, and watched *Countdown*.'

'Every day?'

'Often.'

'Christ.'

Roxy spells it out, 'C H R I S T, Christ, but proper nouns aren't allowed.'

'That bit about the Polish prostitute in your novel,' Jane begins, 'I've always wondered about that—is that true too?'

'Polish prostitute?' Liza says. 'I think I'm going to have to read that book.'

'Don't,' Roxy says. 'It's a bad book.'

'It's not a bad book at all,' Jane says.

'Is it autobiographical?'

'Not all of it.'

'What's it about?'

'Ask Jane, she's read it.'

Jane recounts the plot, a colourful recapitulation of Roxy's childhood. Roxy listens, enthralled.

They drive and eat liquorice non-stop the way girls do. Each time Jane puts a sweet in Roxy's mouth, she feels Jane's fingertips brush her lips. They sing along to the radio; it's a lot like fun.

The car belongs to Roxy; they'll use her credit card to pay for everything. The women are employed by her, yet her power is brittle because the money is finite; Jane has already made that much clear to her. Roxy isn't the person who earned the money, either. She easily could have lived for years on the sales of her book during the short period everyone was interested in it, had it not been, compared to Arthur's income, a 'nice extra', which she used to finance nice extras, like the conservatory. Roxy is out on the razzle with inherited friends she is paying using his money.

They drink wine with their late lunch. Liza, who doesn't have a driver's licence anyway, goes all out.

'I'm not Des,' she grins, and they understand she's making a reference to Roxy's father.

'Who's Des?' Louise asks.

'I'm not,' Liza says.

'I'm the designated driver,' Jane says.

'You're Jane.'

'Jane Des.'

'I'm Louise Rombouts.'

'So, if I've understood correctly,' Liza begins, after her third glass of wine, 'your mother's a sad case because she voluntarily joined a dismal convent and after that she married an idiot who was never home or at some whore's house in Poland ...'

'Yes?'

'And you went to live like a nun in your own convent and you married an old idiot who was never home and who—'

'Who?'

'Fucked his interns.'

'Or the babysitter?'

'No way.'

'No?'

'And why do you drive around in this ridiculous car?'

'Arthur got a suv in the late nineties, before it became hip.'

'Really? So why have you been driving around in ridiculous cars for more than a decade?'

Jane says, 'That's a nice salt-and-pepper set.'

Roxy picks up the slender, glass salt-shaker. It is indeed lovely. 'He did try, but you'd never do a thing like that, right?'

'What do you want to know?'

'Whether he tried?'

'Arthur was a flirt but nothing ever happened.'

'So yes.'

'Jesus Christ,' Jane says. 'Arthur even flirted with the neighbour's dog. It doesn't mean anything.'

'Let's hope so,' Roxy says. She smiles. She gets the salt-and-pepper pots and puts them in her bag, which is hanging over the back of the chair. It's a long time since she's stolen anything. Since being with Arthur she's been able to afford everything, but you never lose the knack. It's easy while you're eating. The main thing is not to be secretive about it. The art is carrying it out as though it's a normal action, part of the meal, like taking a bite of your food. You mustn't disturb people from their routine; they'll only see what they expect to see then.

In the car park, Roxy feels invincible because she's laughed about her bad luck and because she can make things disappear in front of her friends' eyes.

She holds Louise above her head, roaring like a weightlifter. 'I'm a strong mummy.'

'Daddy's a strong mummy too,' Louise says. An old woman shuffling toward them with a walker watches them tenderly.

Roxy lowers her and Louise asks, 'Where's Daddy?'

'Daddy's dead, sweetie,' Jane says. Roxy lifts Louise above her head again and walks away. The woman watches them go.

Roxy is impatient in the car. 'Surprise,' she says, 'for you.' Proudly, she gets the salt-and-pepper set out of her bag. It's like buying a Mother's Day gift with the pocket money you've saved up. The things she steals are more from her than anything she buys with Arthur's money.

'You shouldn't have done that,' Jane says.

IN THE EVENING after dinner, they sit in a bar with a small dance floor, next to the hotel. It's still light outside, and the coloured fairy lights which mark out the dance floor are ridiculous. It's a time of day when you can't imagine people actually dancing in that ludicrous area.

The four of them are sitting on a horseshoe-shaped sofa, the dance floor separating them from the bar. Louise is colouring in beer mats with a wax crayon.

A boy of twenty at most says to Jane, 'You've got beautiful daughters.'

'Thank you.'

'May I offer you something to drink?'

'Sure,' Liza says.

'Same again for everyone?' The boy is already walking to the bar, where his friends are waiting for him expectantly.

Jane gets up. 'I'm too old for this.'

'Can Louise sleep with you tonight?' Roxy asks.

'Yes!' Louise cries, 'a sleepover with Jane!'

Jane hesitates, but says, 'Um … yeah, why not.'

Roxy and Liza drink in harmony, their shared tempo

gradually extending the boundaries, and when Liza dances with the boys that evening, Roxy watches her and she watches Roxy.

Roxy remembers the flirting from her previous life but she's never shared it with a woman before. She remembers parties in barns when she was fifteen. She'd hug every male there but never a girlfriend. The nice thing about this evening is the way she goes to stand next to Liza for a moment and overhears what one of the dopes is whispering in her ear, or what the other is trying in the dark corner of the sofa, and then they hug.

One of the young boys, who has been shooting daggers the whole time and with whom she hasn't exchanged a single word, grabs hold of her later in the evening, pulls her toward him and dances with her. She lets it happen. They don't talk. The deep silence excites her.

At first she doesn't hear the telephone but feels it in her jeans pocket. Without saying a word, she frees herself from her dance partner and gets the phone out of her pocket. She moves sluggishly toward the sofa on the other side of the bar where Liza is chatting to one of the more friendly men. Roxy squeezes in beside them.

'Jane, what's the matter?'

'Sorry,' she says, 'but she's asking for her mother in such a heart-wrenching way, it seemed better to call you.'

'Mummy?'

'Mummy's here, what's the matter, sweetie?'

'Where are you?'

'Mummy's dancing, sweetheart.'

'What is it?' Liza asks.

'Can't sleep,' Roxy says.

'What did you say, Mummy?'

'I was talking to Liza.'

Liza leans against Roxy and sings into the phone, 'Toora, loora, loora. Toora, loora, li. Toora, loora, loora. Hush, now, don't you cry ...'

'What are you singing?' Roxy asks.

'My Granny used to sing that to me ... Ah, toora, loora, loora. Toora, loora, li. Toora, loora, loora. It's an Irish lullaby.'

'Again,' Louise says.

Roxy passes the phone to Liza and Liza sings, 'Toora, loora, loora. Toora, loora, li. Toora, loora, loora. Hush, now, don't you cry. Ah, toora, loora, loora. Toora, loora, li. Toora, loora, loora.' She gives the phone back to Roxy.

'Again,' Louise says.

'You have to sleep.'

'I want a song.'

'Ask Jane to sing.'

'Liza's song.'

Liza is kissing the friendly Belgian.

'Liza can't sing right now.'

'I want Liza's song.'

Roxy taps Liza's shoulder. It takes her a while to feel it, but then she frees herself from the man and turns to Roxy.

'What?'

'She wants your song, Liza.'

'Huh?'

'She wants your song.'

'Liza?' Louise shouts so loudly that Liza hears it too. Roxy gives her the phone.

'Louise? Do you need Mummy to come?' Liza asks. 'I'm not going to sing any more, honey, Mummy'll be right there ... Oh honey, don't cry, I ... just once, all right? ... Just the once ... Toora, loora, loora ...' Liza shunts past

Roxy, off the sofa, '*Toora, loora, li,*' and walks out of the bar singing.

The friendly man looks bewildered.

'Lipstick,' Roxy says, wiping away the faint red stripe next to his mouth.

'Possessive mothers are scary,' she says. 'You should know what your child needs and sometimes that's somebody else.'

He nods.

'Liza's amazing,' Roxy says. 'I trust her. Do you know what that's like? Really trusting someone? I know this is the right thing. I love Liza. Liza's worth her weight in gold—pure gold. That's friendship. She's probably gone to tuck her in. That's what she's like. She's fantastic.'

'Yes,' the man says.

'Do you have any kids?'

He shakes his head slowly.

'They're great, you know, you should get some.'

The sullen man walks over to her.

'You coming?'

He walks off.

'Nice to meet you,' Roxy says to the friendly Belgian.

They leave the bar.

He says, 'I'm in the hotel next door.'

They enter the hotel without speaking, walk along the corridor. Roxy doesn't say she's staying here too. He takes the key card from his breast pocket to open the door.

He kisses her briefly and hastily begins to undress her. When she takes off her shoes, he picks one up.

'What's the matter?'

'Your heels.'

'What's wrong with my heels?'

'They're not high enough.'

'You're too young to already be such a wanker.'

She gets an approving smile and Roxy is pleased that she has amused the wanker.

It's a strange fuck, in which he remains constantly a step ahead of her. For her it all goes just a bit too quick, but she tries her best not to show it. It's more like a competition than sex and she's amazed by how strong such a skinny thing is, how easily he could overpower her if he wanted to. He falls asleep, Roxy doesn't. She dresses quietly and slips out of the room.

Her friends are the only people in the breakfast room. Louise slides out of her chair and runs toward her.

Roxy squats down and rests her forehead against Louise's. 'My heels are exactly the right height.' She picks up her child and presses her to her. She sits down without letting her go. Louise's head rests on her shoulder, her tiny arms tight around her.

Liza shoves Roxy's telephone across the table toward her. 'Where did you disappear to?' She sounds angry.

Roxy asks, 'Did you go and check on Louise?'

'What do you mean?'

'Oh, I thought that's where you went.'

'I stood outside singing and then when I came back, you'd gone. I looked for you everywhere.'

'Oh, sorry. Were you worried?'

'Worried?'

'How was that friendly Belgian of yours?'

'He'd left too.'

Roxy strokes her daughter's head.

'What happened to your wrists?' Jane asks.

Roxy notices the red welts for the first time, where the man held onto her so tightly.

'I went to that man's room for a bit.'

'Jesus, what happened?' Liza asks.

Roxy smiles. 'Nothing bad, he was just a bit rough.'

'But which man was it?'

'The one who looked angry, that skinny one.'

'The creep with the greasy hair?'

'He's not a creep.'

'Well, how nice for you.' Liza yawns.

'Slept badly?'

'Louise came knocking at my door at eight, wanting me to sing her a song. Thanks a mill. Did you have a nice lie in?'

'Come on.'

'What?'

'It's Monday, isn't it?'

'What do you mean?'

Louise says, 'Liza knows some Native American songs.'

'Monday's your day, isn't it?' Roxy says.

'Excuse me?'

'That's what you arranged with Arthur. You always do the Mondays, right?'

It's silent at the table.

'Did I say something odd?'

'Won't you sing the American song?' Louise asks.

'And Thursdays?'

'Well,' Jane says.

'But just say the word, you know,' Roxy says, 'if it's not convenient.'

Liza nods very slowly, as though she hasn't quite understood what was said.

Last night's man is getting into his car in the car park; she doesn't know his name. He's got a totally ridiculous Vauxhall with a racing spoiler. They're just driving off themselves. Roxy had volunteered, 'I'll drive in the morning,' so that she could drink at lunchtime. Now Roxy has seen his car, she regrets it. The pain's not bad but knowing she's fallen for the same trick again is more than she can bear. The others study him attentively.

'I'm sorry, though,' Liza says, 'he really is a creep.'

'He only looks like a creep.'

'He only looks like a creep, talks like a creep, acts like a creep and fucks like a creep. What is it about him that isn't creepy then?'

Jane says, 'If it walks like a duck, quacks like a duck ...'

It's busy on the road; caravans and campers hold up the traffic. They drive behind a car with four bikes on its roof.

'Last night he asked whether he was being too rough for me.'

'Loser,' Liza says. 'And what did you say?'

'I said, "You'd like that, wouldn't you?"'

'Good answer.'

Jane says, 'You also could have said, "Yes, you're hurting me. Stop."'

'You know,' Roxy begins, 'that if you get raped by a gorilla, it's best not to resist? They've got very small penises, so they won't be able to hurt you with them, and if you just let them get on with it, they don't hurt you.'

'Did he rape you?' Jane asks quietly.

'No, of course not.'

'Why did you just come out with all that crap then?'

'Dunno, just thinking.'

'Ugh,' Liza says.

'It's useful to know, isn't it?'

'What's "raped" mean?' Louise asks.

It's quiet in the car. Roxy waits for the question to disappear.

Liza says, 'Someone kissing you when you don't want them to.'

'Oh yes,' Louise says, 'that.'

'Thanks,' Roxy says.

AT LUNCHTIME THEY eat crayfish. It all just fits on the small table, four deep plates of those red creatures, the child having generously been counted as an adult and ordered the same sized portion. Next to the plates, large, green-and-white-checked serviettes, glasses and, of course, wine, chocolate milk, and little red limbs all over the place. They teach Louise how to strip the crayfish. She's too young to be upset by it and grips the creatures more eagerly than the others, worming her fingers deeper into the flesh and rolling the eyeballs between her fingertips. The barbarity contributes to the party atmosphere. The fearless tearing of the bodies shows Roxy there are no boundaries. They are free.

'If only Arthur could see me now.'

Jane had cautiously suggested just getting a sandwich but Roxy had felt depressed at the thought, afraid that the entire party set-up of her new life would collapse at the sight of a cheese sandwich.

Roxy looks at her daughter, her uninterrupted labour. She notices how much stuff is falling next to her plate and onto the floor. She realizes, too, how loudly they are laughing, that the people on other tables are looking, but it's about singing in the round and doing your best to concentrate on singing the right tune, and her tune is called Louise. Being uncivilized, dirty, noisy Dutch people isn't her tune.

'Put them on your plate now,' Liza says to Louise, who has been putting all of her food next to her plate. Roxy merely looks on, an attentive audience member; apparently the food has to go next to the plate. Liza picks up a piece from time to time and wipes Louise's face with a serviette, picking food out of her hair. Roxy sees the child running her greasy fingers through her hair; how easily she gets dirty. She'd be a good weekend father. Maybe it'd be possible on the other days of the week too. She hasn't yet abandoned the idea that she can stay the mother she is now.

'Not so loud, Louise,' Liza says.

'Is she talking too loudly?' Roxy asks.

'We're in a restaurant.'

'Yes,' Roxy says. 'Why is everyone here speaking so quietly? It's making me feel strange.'

'LITTLE FISHIE!' Louise holds up a crayfish.

'Louise,' Roxy says, to appease her friends, 'you have to talk more quietly.'

'Why?'

'I don't know,' Roxy says.

'Because your mother says so,' Liza says.

'Where did you grow up?' Roxy asks Liza. She interrogates her like a job interviewer and doesn't hear anything disturbing: a small village in Groningen. Parents had a bike shop, business is good thanks to electric bike sales. Older sister is a hairdresser, got two kids.

'That's nice for Louise.'

'What?'

'How old are they?'

'Who?'

'Your sister's kids.'

'Two and four.'

'Right in the middle.'

'One two three four five.' Louise sings the only nursery rhyme that Roxy has taught her.

'One, two, three, four, five,

Once I caught a fish alive,

Six, seven, eight, nine, ten,

Then I let it go again.'

'And now eat it,' Liza says.

'Why?'

'Because I say so.'

It's quiet around the table. Roxy feels the tension.

'You know I'll be doing an internship in London in the autumn?'

'Sure.'

'I mean, I won't always ... be there.'

Louise picks up a knife. Roxy does nothing. Liza takes it off her.

'Sure,' Roxy says again.

Liza finds her behaviour inappropriate but Liza is a good egg. She won't let the child down. She'll curse Roxy for it but she'll be there for Louise. Maybe it's unnecessary but the thought calms Roxy down: her child will want for nothing.

Just before they leave the restaurant together, Roxy frees her hand from Louise's and says she has to pop to the toilet, where she stays longer than necessary.

The restaurant is quite dark and outside the light overwhelms her, the bright sunshine. It doesn't match her tipsiness, which belongs to darkness. It reminds her of Mardi Gras, going into a pub in the morning and drinking as though it were deep in the night and when they go outside, greeting the light as though it is a miracle of nature, the midnight sun that shone so erroneously on Brabant.

My God, how beautiful the daylight is and what a drunken idea that someone else would be able to look after the child better than she could. It's a long time since they've had such a lovely summer.

Arthur would have liked the way she is now. She was simply scared, upstairs in that room. What of? Of this? This party?

'Sorry,' she mutters. And, 'Bastard. What a mess, what a wonder.'

'*Vous êtes en voiture?*'

She opens her eyes and lets the sun blind her.

'*Vous êtes en voiture?*'

She looks to the side and sees black spots and then a woman.

'Sorry?'

'*Ma fille est malade.*' The woman points. A girl of around fifteen is vomiting into a rubbish bin next to a bench a short way off. Roxy feels worry creeping into her drunkenness and doesn't want it there.

'*Vous êtes en voiture?*'

Her daughter vomits again.

'*Vous pouvez nous conduire quelque part?*'

Roxy slowly shakes her head. 'Sorry,' she says. She walks away, hurries around the restaurant to the car park. 'I'm not crazy,' she says. 'I'm not crazy,' shaking as though she has narrowly escaped a violent mugging.

The woman is outside a restaurant, for fuck's sake! She

can go inside and ask for help, call a taxi. It's weird. She got here, didn't she? How?

On the motorway, Roxy leans between the two front seats.

'Did you see that mother and daughter in front of the restaurant—those two women?'

'Yes, seedy-looking pair,' Jane says. 'Didn't look too healthy.'

'They wanted a lift.'

'Oh yeah?'

'The car's full,' Liza says.

'Exactly.' Roxy drops back into her seat. Louise yawns unselfconsciously, like a small animal. Cute.

'The girl was ill,' Roxy says.

'Did she say so?' Jane asks.

'Maybe I misunderstood.'

'What did she say then?'

'She was vomiting.'

'Oh yeah?'

'Yeah, she was really ill.'

'Where did they need to go?' Liza asks.

'Dunno, the car's full anyway.'

'But was she really ill?'

Roxy bends forward again. 'I used to help everyone. I gave a street-paper seller a hundred euros once because he said his dog was sick. I fell for everything. And one time ...'

'She was vomiting?' Jane asks.

'What do you mean?'

'So she really was sick, right?'

'Yes. Sure, but well ...'

'What was there to fall for there, then?'

Roxy is alarmed by Jane's tone. 'You know, shit, I mean, isn't it weird asking a total stranger for a lift, they were right in front of a bloody restaurant, she could ask anyone for help, I don't know what the scam is but ...'

'The child was vomiting, you bitch,' Jane says. 'You don't make that up. The woman was panicking; she wasn't thinking straight.'

Roxy doesn't know what to say. She stares through the windscreen, wondering how to rescue the situation, how to get the party atmosphere back and says, 'Please don't call me a bitch. I'm your boss.'

She hopes Jane will laugh but Jane says, 'Oh, is that what this is? A business trip? Should I keep a note of my hours? Liza, are you counting? Are you charging double for overtime, darling?'

'It was a joke.'

'Crap joke.'

'You shouldn't call me a bitch though.'

'Don't get on your high horse. You're a bitch because you didn't help those people.'

'That woman just had a hangover.'

'The kid was twelve or something!'

'Christ, it's not like I ran someone over and drove off or left them behind in the desert. I can't take care of everyone.' Roxy drops back into her seat, as angry as a teenager, disconcerted. She doesn't know how to put things right.

'What's "bitch" mean?' Louise asks.

'I'm one.'

Louise frowns.

'A bitch is ... a bitch is ... when you're not nice.'

'Aren't you nice?'

'I'm nice to you.' They smile at each other; Louise is

satisfied. Roxy takes her hand. Louise's eyes slowly close. Her pupils turn away just before she falls asleep.

They cross the French border.

Jane asks Liza, 'Have you already decided? About your Master's? You were wondering whether to do Fiscal Economics or—'

'Econometrics.'

Clearly they don't want to talk to her. Better to talk about something the bitch knows nothing about.

'Can't you combine them?' Jane asks.

Roxy draws stripes with her finger along the beige leather door. She's tried to love this car. At the beginning, she called it 'the ugly biscuit tin.' Are we going to take the ugly biscuit tin? Arthur didn't think it was very funny so she stopped saying it.

'You have to admit it's a fine car,' he'd said, as recently as this summer.

She said, 'You won't let me call it ugly,' and, 'Sorry, I know you don't like me saying you've forbidden me from doing something.' After that they'd driven in silence for an hour.

She leans forward again between Liza and Jane and says, 'I can make up my own mind about helping people or not, can't I?'

'You can,' Jane says.

'Yes.'

'Yes, and?'

'But we all have to agree, don't we?' Liza says.

Roxy's not used to any kind of disagreement at all. She's a complete stranger to argument. When she was young, she could just do what she liked. There was no enemy. Or the enemy was no competition for her. It was impossible to argue with her parents. One would cry, the other would take off in his truck. She'd tried it with Arthur for a short period of time. In the beginning, she'd walk off swearing sometimes, slamming doors—she was seventeen. But he called her unreasonable and childish so she stopped doing it; she didn't want to be a child. When she'd shouted, 'I hate you,' Arthur had looked insulted and said, 'You can't say a thing like that.' It was impossible to argue with him. He talked to her. His reasonableness would distract her from her anger. They would converse for hours on end, at first on a daily basis, then, imperceptibly, talking turned into negotiating. It was possible to negotiate what she was allowed to feel and what she was allowed to think.

'It's up to you to decide whether you call your mother when you're in that kind of mood, but I just wonder why you do it.'

'It's all right not to like it, but you can't forbid me from—'

'I was only saying—'

'You mustn't think that—'

'It's not about the money you give them but—'

'It *is* about the money.'

'I didn't say that.'

'It's all right to say that.'

'Can't I say what I mean?'

'Will you be out again tonight?'

'Do you mind?'

'I can hardly forbid you ...'

He was a good negotiator but she wanted to win for once, so when they needed another car on top of that ugly suv, Roxy knew that she'd choose. At first he didn't mind her wanting the silly Camaro, that Dinky Toy, but just before they bought it, the man of the house suddenly got interested in high performance cars, or he had Jane look into them. He came home excited one day: Mercedes was producing a high performance car now and it had to be said, Mercedes was the best in everything except pricing, but that wasn't an issue for them. She listened to his arguments with apparent calm, hid herself away in her room and cried—a grown woman, alone in her room, crying about a car. She hadn't done anything like that since her father had threatened to make her wear a pink dress to her first communion party.

'Jane?!' She has shouted right through their conversation. 'Did you and Arthur discuss—'

'What?'

'Sorry, you two were talking.'

'What did you want to ask?'

'I'll ask later.'

'Yes, but what was it?'

'Something about the car. I'll ask you in a minute.' Bloody hell, second mistake of the day. Roxy hates this car, you can barely feel you're driving. You can't even hear it.

Roxy had won back then, with the Camaro, but he'd crashed it and now she's in the back of this fake Chevrolet, next to her sleeping daughter and she takes hold of her tiny floppy hand, she wants to run away from the strange women in the front. The familiar feeling that everyone except Roxy herself is an evil stranger calms her down, everyone except for her and one other person and Arthur has long stopped being that; but maybe she can be it—the child.

ROXY FALLS ASLEEP and when she wakes up again it is raining. In many ways, they've entered a new country: it's greyer, grimier, far from the crayfish and checked serviettes. The radio predicts rainy days and the women in the front make plans. They talk about large hotel chains with swimming pools and saunas, they use words like 'relaxation' and 'just doing nothing'. They are speaking a new, cloudy language, not hers.

When they realize she's awake, Liza asks, 'What do you fancy doing, Roxy?'

'Whatever,' Roxy says, not wanting to upset her enemies now, to avoid confrontation.

They stop in front of an enormous tower block in a suburb, a business hotel. Liza and Jane both want to go to their rooms straight away, spend hours in the bath. Yes, Louise wants to do that too with her mother, for hours.

Roxy says, 'Sure.' Twenty minutes is already an eternity for a child.

Lunch has become an extravagance; they just want to eat sandwiches in their rooms. The word 'sandwich' has fallen—the party is over. Perhaps they'll see each other again in the bar tonight?

'Whatever you want,' Roxy says. She has lifted up her daughter, one hand around the back of her head, pressing it gently against her, as though she must be protected.

The bathroom is large and has mirrors on all four walls.

'Louise everywhere,' Louise says. Roxy turns on the tap and gets undressed without looking in the mirrors.

There's no opportunity for reflection in the bath, she needs all her concentration just to balance that small wet body climbing on her, to catch it when it jumps off her. Roxy manages two bodies and she's good at it. Between the wild wiggling and the sliding, her daughter spends five, maybe six seconds, lying wet and motionlessly on top of her, born again. She can encircle her daughter's small wet head with one hand. Then Louise glides back off her, cooing, causing the water to splash up over the sides. She tries to crawl on top of her, stand, kneel, swim over her. Roxy's hands follow the small body and protect it.

They stand in the room, wrapped up in big hotel towels and Roxy finds it hard to believe that only ten minutes have passed.

'Do you like the hotel?'

'Yes,' Louise says. 'It's my favourite. What are we going to do?'

'We're not going to do anything. We're going to rest.

'I don't want to rest, I want to drive.'

'Drive some more?'

'I want to drive.'

'You want to do the driving?'

'Me drive?'

'Yes, you drive, in the driver's seat, steering.'

'Yes!' Louise cheers. They quickly get dressed again, barely drying themselves, and run with wet hair through the corridors of Louise's favourite hotel.

The two of them sit in the seatbelt, four hands on the wheel. They set off fast, but even then the SUV doesn't make much noise. When Roxy doesn't need to change gear, she wraps her arm around her daughter and it is precisely this protective gesture that makes her feel protected herself. On the motorway, they overtake everyone soundlessly.

'We're going to buy a new car.'

'Where's the yellow car?'

'It's broken.'

'Is the yellow car Daddy's?'

'No, the yellow car's mine. This car is Daddy's.'

'Isn't Daddy coming back?'

'No.'

'Poor Daddy.'

'What about a red car? Shall we buy a red car?'

'I want a yellow one,' Louise says, but of course they can never go back to the same one; he has crashed all the yellow Camaros.

'Your identity isn't your belongings,' Marco said that morning after his death. As though character was much more robust. The person you are can be written off in one smash, just as easily as a car.

A colossal mall looms up alongside the motorway. Roxy takes the exit.

'Look,' she says, 'there are shops in that building, we can shop inside.'

'Inside?'

'They're like shops inside a house.'

'Really?'

Now the ugly shopping mall has become a magical place and of course she wants to go there.

'Open sesame,' Roxy says to the automatic doors. They giggle and run.

They pause for a long time in front of a hardware shop that is selling scented candles and plastic flowers. Louise fingers the plastic roses.

'Do you think they're pretty?'

'Yes,' Louise says, 'they're my favourite.' So Roxy buys a plastic rose for her and Louise carries it proudly through the shopping mall, which is beautiful, of course. There's a sweets section in the chemist's and above a tower of marshmallows and boiled sweets there's a vase containing enormous lollies in the shape of clowns' faces. Roxy squats down next to Louise, their cheeks touching.

'Do you like them?'

'Yes, they're my favourite.'

Roxy's breath mixes with that of her daughter's as they stare at the lollies, and Roxy thinks there's hope for her because she feels something too, even though it's for a lolly with the face of a clown.

They buy a Lego castle; they buy fluorescent slime in a pot; they buy a battery-powered dog. They buy a bouncy ball with a fish and glitter inside it and run and shriek after it through the mall. Roxy knows you shouldn't give children everything they want, but her child doesn't want everything yet. Her mother has introduced the idea that you can buy anything you want and it makes them both crazy with joy.

In the car, they blow up their new big plastic turtle. It is allowed to sit in the front passenger seat.

Back at the hotel, as Roxy is getting out of the car, one of her heels gets stuck. This has never happened before. She tumbles into the car park, her knees hitting something sharp. The pain is torture, but she doesn't make a sound and gets up again without looking at her knee, precisely because she knows it's bad. Blood will be visible, her jeans will be torn, it will scare her and Louise too, so she'll ignore it until Louise is safely inside and busy with something else. She'd just been so good at managing two bodies, now she's managing just one: her daughter's. She walks into the hotel without limping, her daughter's hand in hers and the big blow-up turtle under her arm.

Louise sits on the turtle in front of the television and watches *Tom and Jerry* in French. Roxy carefully takes off her jeans in the bathroom, peels the fabric from the bloody mass and cleans the wound under the shower. The pain doesn't matter as long as the child doesn't notice.

She gets into bed behind her daughter and imagines herself an *über*-mother.

It doesn't last for long because the child wants to eat again.

'I'm hungry.'

Roxy doesn't say anything; she's tired.

'Mummy, I'm hungry.'

Roxy waits; maybe it will stop.

'Mummy, I'm hungry.'

'Yes.'

'What are we going to eat?'

'I don't know.'

'Mummyyyyy.'

'Have you finished your lolly?'

'Can I have the lolly?' Louise has turned around and gives her a radiant smile.

'Yes, let's have the lolly. Get it out of my bag.'

Louise eats the giant lolly that is bigger than her own head and Roxy eats a whole bag of crisps. *Tom and Jerry* has finished. *Teenage Mutant Ninja Turtles* begins.

'Do you like this?'

'Yes.'

'It's not scary?'

'It's not scary.'

Roxy calls her father. The telephone rings and rings.

'Wim speaking.' There's noise, music.

'Wim? It's Roxy.'

'Hey doll.'

'Hi Wim, is my dad there?'

'Hang on.'

'Hey chick.'

'Where are you?'

'I'm at The Pump, hang on a mo', I'll go outside.' Someone calls her father's name. 'Just play on,' he says.

'Pool?'

'Snooker.'

'So you're still there?'

'Uh?'

'I thought you'd have gone home already.'

'We're looking after the place. Marcel was just here.'

'Marcel?'

'Nice bloke; nothing wrong with him.'

'No? Is he fairly okay? With everything?'

'You don't have to worry about that.'

'No, right?'

'Spent the night, didn't he.'

'Christ, you're kidding.'

'Come on missy, who's looking after the place, you or me?'

'You don't have to housesit. You can just go home, you know.'

'The garden gates don't shut properly, you know that?'

'Yeah, I need to get them repaired.'

'I'll sort it, just needs a bit shaved off them.'

'Thanks.'

'Where are you? Is it nice?'

Roxy says nothing.

'Are you still there?'

'I don't think they like me.'

'Pair of bitches, ain't they, if they don't like you. Tell them I said that.'

'Go back to Wim, I'll call you later.'

Roxy picks up her child, lolly and all.

'TV,' she says.

'Yeah yeah.'

She puts her in bed, pulls the covers over her legs. At last Louise falls asleep in front of a telesales advert for irons.

Roxy takes the lolly out of her hands, carefully freeing her hair where she is lying on the clown's face.

She turns on the baby monitor, even though she's almost certain she won't get a signal in the bar, but no one needs to know.

The monitor starts beeping in the corridor already, out of range. Roxy turns it off and takes the lift downstairs.

Liza and Jane are sitting at the bar. That 'maybe' of theirs had seemed like mere politeness to her, of course they didn't want to see her again today, but now they are there and for a moment there's a glimmer of hope that the hostility she felt was a spectre, a figment of her imagination. Arthur had suggested this sometimes when she'd been afraid of someone, but Arthur not seeing enemies didn't mean anything. No man could be more astonished when someone said he'd offended them.

His face expressionless, he'd say, 'You might have a problem with me but I don't have one with you.'

With elaborate politeness, Roxy asks her friends how their afternoon was, and listens silently to their babbling conversation, grateful that she is allowed to sit with them. They aren't far from Paris.

Jane says, 'It's never taken me so long to drive that bit as with you.' It's true, they're travelling at the speed of toddlers, stopping every time something interests them. They take ages to drink each cup of coffee, they spend hours over lunch. Liza wants to go into Paris tomorrow, wants to see the Louvre. Roxy feels immediate resistance to any kind of museum. You're not allowed to run there, no squealing, but mainly she's afraid of the beauty. Not the kind of beauty that she and Louise attribute to things, but that ostentatious display that crushes them and leaves them dumbfounded.

'The Louvre,' Jane says. 'Always pleasant.'

'I hate museums,' Roxy says, but no one believes her.

'I'll have to call Ludovic then,' Jane says. 'Friend of mine in Paris. I can't go to Paris without calling Ludovic.'

'He doesn't have to know you've been to Paris.'

Jane is speechless for a moment.

Roxy says, 'It doesn't even occur to you, that you can keep quiet about it?'

'I *want* to call Ludovic.'

'Didn't *that* occur to you?' Liza asks Roxy now.

Another faux pas. Roxy stiffens but Liza leans against her. She feels the still-damp hair against her cheek.

'Do you mind if I get an early night?'

'I won't manage that long myself,' Jane says.

Roxy's gaze glides over the men at the bar. She doesn't expect any of them to make her truly happy but she can't help looking, the way you'd absent-mindedly inspect a fridge because you want something to eat, even though you know there isn't anything you fancy, and then you still end up putting a gherkin or a stale chunk of cheese in your mouth.

Liza tilts her head and asks, 'Did you know the other woman?'

'Who? Marcel's wife?'

'Marcel?'

'The undertaker,' Jane says.

'No, I mean the woman Arthur was in the car with.'

'Met her a couple of times.'

'Do you mind me asking?'

Naturally the answer is 'yes', but Roxy shrugs. 'Would you want to know everything?'

'I wouldn't,' Liza says, 'but not long ago you were saying you were the kind of person who can't help looking at motorway accidents, that, on the contrary—'

'Did I say that?'

'Yes.'

'I thought I knew everything. Is that naïve?'

'Who are you asking?'

'Do you think that's stupid?'

A short man comes over to join them. He says, 'I heard you speaking Dutch.'

Liza and Roxy smile warmly; Jane keeps a poker face.

'Where are you from?'

'The Netherlands,' Jane says.

He ignores the jibe. 'Holiday or work?'

'Holiday,' Roxy says, 'and you?'

'I've been to a football match.'

'Shouldn't you be singing in a pub somewhere or something?' Liza asks.

'No,' he says, 'it's my job. I'm a scout.'

'So you don't play yourself?'

'Used to play, dodgy knees.'

'Were you good?' Liza asks.

'Good enough,' he offers his hand. 'I'm David.' He shakes their hands, they're forced to introduce themselves.

Jane says, 'I'm off to bed.'

'Am I boring you?' David asks.

Jane blushes, which is unusual for her. She doesn't like to be rude.

'No,' she says, 'I have to call home.'

'And you?' he looks at Roxy, 'do you need to call home too?'

'Not me, I'm a free person.'

'And you, David?' Jane asks with her sweetest smile, 'Don't you have to call home?'

'No, mine go to bed early.'

He gets out his telephone and shows them a picture of his wife and young son. A pretty blonde in a summer dress on a terrace, a baby wearing a football shirt on her lap.

'Three months today.'

'Oh, what a cutie,' Roxy says. 'I've got a three-year-old girl.'

'Yes,' Jane says. 'Attractive woman.' She stands up.

Liza says, 'I have to make a call too.'

'You're not going to leave me here alone, are you?' David asks.

Roxy doesn't leave him.

David asks, 'Is there anything I can do for you?'

'What do you mean?'

'Is there anything in particular you like?'

Roxy's hand had just been clutching her glass on top of the bar, but now her fingers let go, as though somebody has hit her hand with a small hammer, reminding her muscles to relax.

'You can ask me anything.'

'Anything?' She has to gulp.

'What would you like me to do?'

Her body slackens. Only her eyes are still alert, weighing up the man opposite her, ironic smile, nice teeth.

'Well?'

Saying it is worse than doing it. 'I'm not ... that good ... at theoretical things.'

'If we just say it out loud,' he says, 'I'll know what the programme is.' He smiles. He's enjoying this, as cheeky as a little boy. 'What do you want then? What do you want me to do to you?'

The last thing Roxy wants to be is a coward. 'I want you to kiss me.'

'Where should I kiss you?'

'First my mouth.'

'And then?'

'Why do I have to say everything?'

'Oh,' he says cheerfully, 'do you want me to tell you what I feel like doing?'

'Yes.'

'Okay, so *you* want me to tell you what I feel like doing?'

To persuade herself that this is not happening to her, that she's in control, she says, 'Yes, David, I want you to tell me what you feel like doing.'

'I'll put you on the table and open your legs wide. Will you let me?'

'Yes.'

'I'll kiss you. Will you let me?'

She smiles.

'I'm hard.'

'Now?'

His hand covers his crotch. 'And later.'

'Later?'

'What will you let me do?'

'Later?'

'In my room. What will you let me do to you?'

'Don't you need to call home?'

'I just told you that they are asleep.' He smiles sweetly and says, 'You know how it is. I don't have anything to hide from you.'

'Not from me.'

'You can just say it.'

'What?'

'What you want me to do to you.'

'Now?'

'Come.'

He goes to pick up the baby monitor from the bar, but she is quicker.

In his room, he kisses her, his hand up her skirt. There isn't a table he can lift her onto. Roxy doesn't have any condoms and doesn't feel like asking. It doesn't matter.

His fingers are in her and her hand is around his cock and she's incredibly touched by how well two strangers can take care of each other, it must have something to do with love and she looks at him, he's got such beautiful light eyes. She wants to say, 'I love you,' but she doesn't. She knows what people consider normal, so she keeps to herself the fact she knows how you can get rid of the strangeness between two people.

Roxy listens at the bedroom doors to see if anyone is awake. The sound of a television is coming from Jane's room.

Jane is sitting on the bed, she doesn't turn off the TV, but she does turn down the sound. She's wearing glasses.

'What are you watching?'

'A film.'

'Have you spoken to your friend? Ludovic, wasn't it?'

'Yeah, this afternoon. We're seeing him tomorrow.'

'Great.'

On the television screen, a large group of people are eating at a table in a garden.

'Do you want to carry on watching?'

'There's not much on.'

'Did you really have to call home?'

'You can sit down if you want.'

Roxy sits down next to Jane on the big bed.

'I don't know your girlfriend's name.'

'Oh, don't you?'

'You always say, "my girlfriend."'

'Cynthia.'

'She's much younger, isn't she?'

'Yes.' Jane gets up and turns off the TV.

'Did you have fun with that footballer?'

'Scout, he's a scout.'

'Scout.'

'I went up to his room for a bit.'

'Oh, did you? I've made tea, do you fancy a cup?'

'Lovely.'

She pours tea into a water glass and passes it to Roxy. She sits down on a chair facing the bed.

'Those glasses suit you,' Roxy says.

'Do you think?'

'You always look nice.'

'What's this?'

'What?'

'Are you flirting with me?'

'I was only saying you always look nice. That's allowed, isn't it?'

Jane stares at the floor and says quietly, 'Thanks.'

'You're not angry with Arthur?' Roxy asks.

'No,' Jane says, 'I'm not angry with him. I miss him.'

'And surely you think I should miss him too?'

'You asked about *my* feelings.'

'Are you angry with me?'

Jane sighs.

Roxy feels hot; it's partly the tea's fault. She stands up, sets the glass down on the bedside table. 'Sorry, I'm not making much sense. I'm tired. I need to go to bed.'

'Roxy.'

Her hand is already on the doorknob, she opens the door, tries out a sincere smile, turning toward Jane. 'I'm tired, I'm going to bed.' She's about to leave.

'Roxy, stay for God's sake.'

Roxy lets the door fall closed again and says, 'You *are* angry.'

'I don't have to stand up and cheer every time you fuck some wacko!'

'What do you mean, wacko? He was a really nice man! You're just being a snob.'

'A really nice man?! In what way, Roxy? What was nice about him?'

'…'

'What?!'

'I don't have to justify myself to you.'

'I'm just asking you what was nice about that man.'

'If I say he was …'

'What?'

'He smelled nice.'

Jane is silent.

'Smell is very important.'

'Why can't you just say you miss Arthur?'

'Do you really want me to?'

'Fucking hell, Roxy.'

'But why are you so angry?' And then Roxy starts crying like a child. 'I don't want you to be angry, I just don't want you to be angry.'

'I'm not …'

'What do I have to do to stop you being angry? Should I say I miss him? I don't mind saying that I miss him if you tell me how to. How do I do that? I've lost everything—all those years—I can't find him. I just don't know how.'

'Roxy …'

'I want to miss him, but I just don't want you to be angry.' She's still crying. 'I just don't want you to—'

'SHUT UP!'

Roxy is so shocked, she shuts up. She wipes away her tears. 'Sorry.' She opens the door.

'Roxy.'

'Sorry.'

'Don't forget your baby monitor.'
Roxy turns back and takes it from her.
'But it's not switched on,' Jane says.
'Oh.'
'Oh?'
'Won't have reception here anyway.'
'The bloody thing's not even on.'
'I'll go and have a look.'
'Has it been off all evening?'
'Jane, I can't talk now, I have to go to my daughter.'
'The bloody thing isn't even on, Roxy! It's not even on.'
'I'm off! Yeah? I'm off already.'

She throws the monitor into the corner of her hotel room. Louise groans and sits up.
'Go back to sleep.'
'Mummy?'
'Go to sleep, for God's sake.'
'Can't sleep.'
'That's not true, you were asleep, weren't you?'
'I want a song.'
'One, two, three, four, five, once I caught—'
'I want Liza's song.'
'—a fish alive.'
'Liza's song.'
Roxy cries. 'Go to sleep, for God's sake, please!'
'Mummy, don't cry.'
Roxy undresses and climbs into bed with her daughter. She lies behind her, wraps an arm around her and tries to lie still. Louise falls asleep.
Roxy pictures the fabric of life, the pile of papers on the kitchen table. She can't be running away from a pile of papers, can she? Any idiot can do that, so she can too.

'One year,' Jane had said, 'at the most, if you live frugally.' The SUV will have to be sold and they'll need to get a cheaper car in its place; a smaller house would be better. She'll have to get a job. She doesn't have any skills.

'You have to let me sleep,' she says to Louise in the morning but Louise is hungry and doesn't want her lolly any more.

'I'm so tired,' Roxy says, crying. She is expecting another touching 'Mummy, don't cry' but Louise thumps the pillow and screams.

'All right, all right,' Roxy says. 'I'll stop, but hush now.'

Louise doesn't quieten down. Roxy sits up but doesn't touch the hysterical child next to her.

'I want Daddy,' Louise shouts.

'I get that,' Roxy says in a toneless voice, without moving. 'Come here.'

'No!' Louise shrieks.

Roxy knows full well how to stop this. She has to get up, take charge of the situation. Be firm. Be loving. Instead of getting up, she thinks about the expression 'to take care of someone' and how you have to 'take care', beware, how she might write something about that, but that's the last thing she wants to do, write. The last thing she wants is to spend hours in the same place. She has to get away, get a heavy goods licence at last. Her father always said she was a good driver. Louise screams louder. Maybe just leave her. She'll run out of steam, surely?

Roxy calculates how many months she's got until the child has to start school, how much time she's got to become a stable mother who makes packed lunches in the morning; you always have to have bread in the house, bread every day, and you really need a big freezer. She needs to remember that if they move to a smaller place, those smaller freezer compartments always freeze shut. Louise doesn't calm down. Someone bangs on the wall in the room next to theirs.

Roxy lays a hand on Louise's back. 'Hush now.' The child shakes her hand off. 'Everything will be fine.'

'I'm hungry!'

'Yes, let's eat.' Roxy stands up and puts on a pair of jeans and tries not to cry and also not to sit down or maybe just for a moment. Louise continues to cry. More banging on the wall.

'I want Daddy!'

Roxy sits next to Louise on the bed and stops moving. It's not actually that difficult. Once you've let your child scream for the first time without doing anything, you can just sit there calmly. The longer it takes, the calmer you become. This must be what drowning is like: apparently you grow numb and accept the inevitable. She sinks down some more, closes her eyes, but just before she's about to fall asleep, Louise screams even louder, making her start.

She calls Liza.

'What's going on there? What's the matter with Louise?'

'We're not okay. I'm sorry, you have to help me.'

When Roxy lets in Liza, Louise gets straight out of bed and runs to her. Liza lifts her up.

Louise turns her head briefly toward her mother, holds out her hand and says, 'Bye bye.'

'You look terrible,' Liza says.

'I'm sorry. I can't cope. I didn't know what to do. She wouldn't stop crying and ... I just couldn't cope. Just for a while, mind. Did I wake you up?'

'No, we were already up.'

'Jane too?'

'We wanted to leave in time, otherwise there's such a long queue at the museum.'

Her friends take their time in the museum. They leisurely discuss what they see, point out details to the child and tell her stories. Roxy walks behind them, turning in circles and figures of eight, like the bored teenager of the family, until she finally stops in front of the painting of Napoleon in full regalia, standing amongst a group of sickly, naked people; it's too strange not to take a closer look.

'Napoleon visiting the plague-stricken at Jaffa,' Jane says.

Napoleon is touching the boils of one of the plague victims.

'What a strange painting,' Roxy says. Louise points to the sickly, naked bodies lying in the foreground of the picture, almost voluptuously, and asks, 'Are they sleeping or dead?'

'They're poorly,' Liza says.

Roxy wants to reach out, she wants to touch the white, painted flesh, feel the squirming bodies. Arthur's twisted body emerging from the wreckage unexpectedly springs to mind, the soft flesh of his belly, his skinny legs. Did he feel any pain? Please let him not have felt any pain. Roxy feels her arms wanting to pick him up, protect him, and comfort him, but how can she take his body in her arms if someone else is already holding it?

'Are you all right?' Liza asks.

She pictures the contorted metal that enclosed him and her. Did they cut them out? Does she really need to ask all of this? Is it necessary? Must she know every-thing?

'Are you okay?'

'I miss the Camaro.'

They eat chocolate cake sitting at a small, round table in a luxury brasserie. Jane sends a message to that friend of hers to say where he can find them. That friend of hers is making Roxy nervous—a secret weapon that has been announced with an exact time of arrival.

'He's French then?'

'No,' Jane says, 'he's Dutch, but he lives here.'

'Does he work here?'

'Retired. He couldn't stand the Netherlands.'

'But he can stand France?' Liza asks.

'Yes.'

'Why?'

'Because it's not Holland.'

'What's he got against Holland?' Roxy asks.

'He doesn't have anything against Holland but ... how can I put it? It's like living in a house you always got beaten up in. It might be a pretty house, but you still can't live there anymore.'

'I get that,' Liza says, sounding serious. They carry on eating the chocolate cake, bringing an end to the topic of conversation. Roxy finds it difficult joining in with this new, poetic way of talking, this innuendo. Her cake is long finished.

'What happened, then?'

'What didn't happen?' Jane says.

Have they always talked like this? They carry on calm-ly eating with awkward, tiny forks and slight smiles on their faces. They've left banality behind, explicitness, indifference, toughness, sharpness. Somewhere half-way through the journey, they must have embraced that Flemish indirectness that Roxy finds so impossible to understand.

'You should use a fork,' Liza says to Louise who is eating the chocolate cake with her hands.

'I want her back.'

'What?'

'I don't mind if she eats with her hands. These forks are impossible. Come here, sweetheart.'

Louise clambers onto her lap. Louise eats chocolate cake using her hands and Roxy licks the crumbs from her cheeks. Louise laughs.

'There he is,' Jane says.

The man is older than Jane, well into his seventies, and walks with a stick. He's wearing lightweight trousers and a shirt, neither of them new or eye-catching but they are immaculate, making Roxy instantly feel grubby with her chocolatey child. Here's a man they mustn't touch. Jane stands up, cool and composed. He quietly rests his stick against the table and they hug each other, at length and without embarrassment. He closes his eyes. When they let go, they look at each other and say each other's names.

Can't they just be done with it? Roxy thinks when they repeat the ritual. Liza watches with a smile. When they let go, it's their turn. They receive a firm handshake, are studied and their names repeated. It's all love and friendship and geniality and manners. It's unbearable.

Ludovic hasn't had lunch yet; they mention eggs and toast. Ludovic's shirt has slightly worn cuffs and yet it's a good quality shirt, or once was. She thinks of old houses and remembers once asking her mother whether everyone used to be rich in the past because all the old houses were so big and beautiful. Her mother explained to her that only the rich houses lasted; turf huts didn't last for centuries. Ludovic is a rich old house.

'What are you up to?' Jane asks.

'I read a lot,' Ludovic says, 'and I've taken up a bit of drawing again. I've got my clubs. What about you? Still busy with your film producer?'

Jane shakes her head. 'There's so much to tell. A lot has happened.'

Roxy experiences a perverse sense of curiosity. How is Jane going to convey the news?

'We've come on an impulsive holiday: me and Roxy and Louise and Liza. Roxy is Arthur's wife.' Then she looks at Roxy, passing her the baton.

'Oh!' he says, delighted. 'How nice. I've never met Arthur, unfortunately.'

'You're never going to,' Roxy says.

'Sorry?'

'Do you know that magazine you get in waiting rooms, *My Secret*?'

He nods enthusiastically.

'They've got a feature called, "In brief in the newspapers, in depth in *My Secret*." My life can be summarized like the headline of one of those articles: "MY HUSBAND WAS KILLED IN THE ARMS OF HIS MISTRESS."' She smiles.

Ludovic gives Jane a questioning look now, longing for a translation into cautious, affectionate language.

'Arthur died in a car crash,' she says softly, 'at the beginning of the month.'

He slaps his hand to his mouth, almost theatrically. Roxy can't stop giggling.

'Why are you laughing?' Louise asks.

'I'm not.'

'You are.'

'I made a mistake,' she whispers.

'Why are you whispering, Mummy?'

'Mistake.'

'How awful, my dear,' Ludovic says. Now she has to wait until the cultured man who never met Arthur has processed the news of Arthur's death. She looks past him to the window, the Louvre, the rooms she ran away from, escaping beauty, running right into the arms of kindness itself. She cautiously looks at the man again: no change, damp eyes, dismayed expression.

This is taking too long. She gets up with Louise in her arms. 'You haven't been to the loo yet.'

She squats down, her back to the toilet door, her daughter on the toilet. Louise looks at her without blinking as she pees. A thing like this is finite. One day it will have become normal. How long will Louise still belong to her? Can she avoid situations like this morning's?

Roxy hears footsteps in the corridor and recognizes Liza's heels. She stiffens and holds her breath but Louise's face brightens and she shouts out, 'We're in here!'

'Shhh!' Roxy says, her finger to her lips. Louise gives her a look of incomprehension.

'It's a secret,' Roxy says, 'us being here.'

Louise beams. 'Yeah!'

They wait breathlessly as Liza enters the toilet sink area.

Louise cries, 'It's a secret where we're hiding. You can't find us!'

Roxy lets her head hang.

'What's the matter, Mummy?'

'Roxy?'

'Mummy?'

'Roxy, are you all right?'

She looks up. 'Everything's all right.'

'I didn't want to leave you alone,' Liza says.

Leave her alone? She's just sitting on the toilet. The words alarm her and fear rises up like an insight, an alertness that will save her from approaching danger.

It's not the first panic attack in her life. Arthur was familiar with them.

Once he had continued to ask the question, 'What exactly are you frightened of?'—searching for a concrete object of terror that could be rendered innocuous with questions and answers. When Arthur stopped asking the question after a few years, Roxy thought he'd understood that the point was that she was afraid of an unknown danger. The only thing you know is that it is coming, but you never know how or from which side. Now it dawns on her that Arthur hadn't understood, he'd given up. He'd given up on her.

Louise unrolls half the toilet roll. As long as she's busy doing that, they can stay put and she can run through her options.

What are you frightened of then? If only there had been a concrete danger, God only knows, she'd like nothing better. She wants to fight; she's no coward. Please don't let her be a coward.

Of course she knows she's afraid of being left alone with the child, that the only thing expected of her will be just to get through the day: sticking plasters on grazes, making sandwiches, not being anything special, and being alone. He once had her believe that together they were more special than the rest, a feeling it's easy to believe in when you are seventeen, one that should have been replaced by something else in time. The feeling did fade over the years but nothing turned up in its place.

There has to be a better form of misery than this, something that calls for action, combat. Not night after night of being alone with the fly, without Arthur's voice to tell her she's imagining it. Was that a lie too? That her fears were imaginary?

Roxy soaps her hands at length because Liza is standing next to her.

'Give them a chance to chat,' Liza says. 'They've been friends for thirty years or so.' Liza is making small talk and trying to forge a connection to parallel Jane and Ludovic's. Roxy has to play her cards right, not give anything away, keep her options open.

'That's lovely,' Roxy says. 'Such a long friendship.'

'Sweet guy.'

'Really sweet,' Roxy says.

Roxy washes Louise's hands.

'It's sad,' Liza says.

You're not safe from emotion anywhere. Roxy lifts Louise up to the hand dryer and dries their hands. The noise makes conversation impossible. Louise squirms free.

'Hot,' she says.

Roxy washes her hands, immediately realizing she's already done that.

'Mummy.'

'Mummy,' Louise tugs at her leg, 'Mummy.'

'I can hear you.'

'Then you have to say "yes."'

'What is it now? Can't you just say what you want?'

'You have to say "yes."'

'yes.'

'Look, a spider.' She points to a corner of the ceiling.

'Look, then.'

'I am looking.'

'Roxy?' Liza lays a hand on her arm.

'Roxy?'

'yes.'

Liza pulls her hand back in shock.

'Sorry. That wasn't meant for you.'

'Who was it meant for, then?'

'I was mistaken.'

'Can I do anything for you?'

'Sometimes I think I can't breathe here. With all these people around.'

'You can't breathe when other people are around?'

'It feels like being underwater, you can't keep it up forever.'

'I think you need to get some help.'

Roxy dries her hands again. 'Help.'

'Huh?'

'Get help?'

'Yes.'

The dryer stops.

'Okay,' Roxy says.

'Yes?'

'Yes.'

Liza hugs her, satisfied. Roxy almost says, *glad to assist.*

Ludovic and Jane are sitting opposite each other, blind to anyone else, like lovers.

Jane is crying. 'Sometimes he'd call me ten times a day.'

Louise looks worried and rests a hand on Jane's lap. 'Oh, poor darling.' These are the words her mother uses when she's hurt herself.

Jane pulls her, grinning, onto her lap, cuddles her and Louise laughs just a little too loudly, happy that the tears have stopped. Ludovic is touched.

'Have you already ordered?' Roxy asks.

'Yes,' Ludovic says.

'What are we drinking, guys? White or red? Jane, you're driving this afternoon? Wine Liza? Ludovic? You'll join us, won't you?'

A brief exchange of glances between he and Jane.

'No, I still don't,' he says. 'Hasn't Jane told you we met in rehab?'

'Rehab?'

'Fifteen years ago last summer.'

'What were you doing in rehab?' Roxy asks Jane, the naïvety of her question hitting her immediately. For a moment, she'd imagined her a PA to the director, or whatever kind of job you get in an alcohol clinic; in any case, she saw her as the cool and collected Jane she knows. Now she rewinds the days in her head and thinks back to their evenings, dinner, lunches. Has she seen her drink? Not that she can remember. How is it possible she didn't notice? She blushes because she already knows the answer: she didn't really see Jane.

'I'm the designated driver,' Jane says, 'I'm always Des.'

'Jane Des,' Louise says, as though she's saying, *even I knew that, Mummy, pay attention!*

'I didn't know,' Roxy says. 'Did you?' she asks Liza.

Liza nods cautiously. 'I thought ... you knew.'

Everyone smiles. Even Louise is smiling, all of them acting as though this doesn't matter.

'So we're drinking alone,' Roxy says.

'Yes,' Jane says. 'You've been drinking alone for weeks.'

The wine tastes illicit and it makes her drink more quickly.

Ludovic and Jane want to talk about Arthur's death but it's impossible if she doesn't join in the conversation.

When Jane says, 'I couldn't help taking care of him,' she is compelled to cast a glance at Roxy, who remains aloof. When Jane says she knew everything about Arthur, or thought she did, she stutters. Roxy is getting in the way. She has to join in or leave.

Ludovic tries to involve her.

'You're a writer, aren't you?'

'Yes, three books. One trashy, successful book, and two humourless monstrosities, but well, I'd already signed the contracts.'

'Humourless?' Liza asks.

'Yes, that's what they wrote in any case.'

'But did you think they were humourless?' Ludovic asks.

'Yes, they were humourless, but I meant them to be. It was wonderful doing without humour for a bit.'

'So you were happy?' Ludovic asks.

'You'd think so, wouldn't you?' Roxy says, roaring with laughter, Louise on her lap, her knees moving upward.

'Horsey!' Louise cries.

Roxy sings, 'This is the way the lady rides, the lady

rides, the lady rides,' her knees bouncing rhythmically, 'this is the way the lady rides on a cold and frosty morning.' Louise shrieks as she's bounced upward. 'And down into the ditch!' Roxy spreads her legs and lets Louise sink to the floor, Louise screaming. Other customers turn their heads.

'Again!'

Ludovic hugs her when they say goodbye. It's strange moving past a male head, without any devouring or being devoured. It feels like an indiscretion, ending up with your head so casually resting on somebody else's shoulder.

It's hazy, the sun is no longer so bright, but it won't be long before the summer gets back on its feet.

Roxy carries Louise until they reach the car; the strength has returned to her arms. She waits until they are on the motorway to say, 'Arthur never told me you went to rehab.' It sounds like an accusation.

'Can I do anything about that?'

'Didn't you want me to know?'

'Sorry, I never even thought about it.'

'He told me fucking everything,' Roxy says, 'I even know what your favourite food is.' It's quiet in the car. They are following a truck, slowly. 'Well no, not everything,' Roxy says.

'You're angry with Arthur, not with me,' Jane says.

Roxy forces herself to calm down. 'It's just weird. I thought we—'

'Yes, what?' Jane asks. 'Tell me, Roxy, what did you think?'

'I thought we shared things.'

'Yes, we all thought that, but just because he had

secrets, it doesn't make everything lies, does it?'

'I wasn't talking about Arthur, I was talking about us.'

Liza leans forward and asks Jane, 'Are you going to overtake that truck or not?'

'Are you driving or am I?'

'I really can't picture it,' Roxy says. 'You, drunk.'

'No,' Liza says, 'me neither.'

Jane suddenly shoots into the left-hand lane causing the car behind them to brake and toot its horn. 'Because I'm the very picture of self-control?'

'Watch out,' Liza says.

Jane accelerates, forcing the car in front to move to the right. 'Because everyone feels safe with me?' She flashes the next car, which doesn't move aside in time. 'Because I have to be your mother?'

They are driving at 160 kilometres an hour now and the needle on the speedometer goes higher. She overtakes a car on the left.

'Stop it,' Liza says.

'Go Jane, go Jane,' Roxy says.

'No!' Louise cries.

'Racing is fun, sweetie.'

'Don't want to race!'

'It's all right, sweetie, look, we're overtaking everyone.'

Louise is crying.

'Sweetheart, you don't have to cry.'

'Jane, stop it,' Liza shouts, 'the kid's really upset!'

Jane shoots into the exit lane, drives to the car park next to a petrol station and slams on the brakes.

Louise shouts, 'Out of the car!'

Outside, Liza picks her up.

Jane walks off and stands a short distance away, smoking a cigarette.

'Mummy's angry,' Roxy says.

Liza isn't amused. She turns away from Roxy.

The sun is high in the sky, all the clouds have disappeared. Summer is back. Steam rises from the fields. Roxy thinks, *I'm not the right person for a frightened child.*

Liza puts Louise down and kneels on the verge. 'Look, a ladybird.'

'Come on,' Roxy says, 'let's go buy sweets.'

Louise doesn't respond. She sits down on the verge next to Liza, who is allowing the ladybird to walk along her arm.

'Do you want him on your hand?'

'Don't dare,' Louise says.

'Rubbish,' Roxy says, 'you're not afraid of insects.'

Louise sits on her hands. 'I am too.'

'Come on,' Roxy says, 'let's buy some chocolate.'

'No,' Louise says.

'Don't be silly, come with me.'

'I'm not silly. I'm not going with you.'

Louise is angry.

Roxy slowly walks off, giving the child ample opportunity to call her back or run after her, but she doesn't follow.

Roxy turns back again and studies from a distance her daughter, who only has eyes for Liza.

'Come on now,' Roxy says gently, 'I need you.' Can you ask a child that?

Roxy walks past the petrol station, as far as the parking area for trucks. She wanders between the trucks and imagines that one of them is hers, with a cabin she can climb into and her own bed. She picks out a black Renault Magnum and leans against the cabin, one foot up against a wheel, nonchalantly trying it out and making it hers.

Across the road, a man gets out of a truck with a Czech number plate. He stands coolly next to his truck. He has a beard and it's hard to guess his age. He makes a gesture of invitation with his head, very simple, like a person you know wordlessly saying, *come here a minute.*

She detaches herself from the truck and almost takes a step but then stops. Jane would disapprove. She takes a step anyway—that isn't a good reason to control herself—and then another step. She can hear Jane saying, 'Don't let me stop you.' Then she shakes her off and carries on walking.

The man isn't that old—her age. Once he gets home again, he'll shave his beard off, they do that. She hasn't yet reached him when he opens his cabin door. She smiles at his haste and shakes her head.

If the truck behind her was hers, she could go back to it whenever it suited her. She can do it too, make friends easily. It wouldn't be a bad life.

She takes off her sunglasses. The man gets his wallet out of his jeans pocket and only then does she realize what he's thinking.

Poised, she puts her sunglasses back on. She's afraid. She carefully takes a step back and walks away, first slowly, then faster.

'Hey!' the man calls after her. 'Hey!' And then she runs until she's reached the other side of the petrol station with the families and the picnic tables. Liza and Louise are still sitting on the verge.

The summer she spent with her father, she did everything at a run. She was frightened as a thirteen-year-old in the car parks; she'd forgotten that. She described everything in her novel except the fear, but back then there was somewhere to run at least.

She sits down at a picnic table with a view of Liza and Louise. They look like each other.

Roxy calls her father.

'Where are you? Are you having a laugh?'

'A laugh?'

'Enjoying the sea?'

'We've just passed Paris.'

'What? Are you on foot?'

'How are things there?'

'I'm helping Wim plaster a wall.'

'So you're still there?'

'It's a lovely house but way too big for just two of yous.'

'Hey, Dad.'

'Yes?'

'It was fun, wasn't it, that summer?'

'We had a bloody laugh, doll.'

'Why didn't we do it more often?'

'You were always with some lad, kiddo. You never wanted to go.'

'You could have made me.'

Her father is silent.

'Dad?'

'A man can't come home four times a year and then go calling the shots, right?'

'No.'

'That's what I said.'

'Are you angry?'

'Are you going to bellyache or were you calling for a nice chat?'

'How's Mum?'

'*Knees up Mother Brown, knees up Mother Brown,*' her father sings.

Roxy joins in, '*Under the table you must go.*'

'It's mainly been the wine since we got here.'

'The top ones?'

'No, she said the ones at the bottom were much nicer.'

'Shit.'

'Wim wanted me to tell you he's writing a book.'

'Wim?'

'"Erotic Stories by the Washing-machine Repairman."'

'Christ. Shouldn't you be hitting the road sometime soon?'

'That's man's got the gift of the gab!'

'Any work in the offing?'

'Don't you worry about that, Roxy.'

'Has Marcel gone?'

'That was just the one night, kiddo.'

'We had fun, didn't we, that summer?'

'Is something wrong?'

'Will you come and get me?'

'What?'

She doesn't reply; he can let it pass.

'Do I need to come and fetch yous?' *Yous.*

'Yes?'

'What'll I do with your Mum?'

'You're asking me?'

'Sometimes I think she drinks too much.'

'You're kidding me, right?'

He laughs.

'Drop Mum off at home and drive here?'

'I'll finish that wall with Wim and hit the road tonight.'

They find a hotel on the edge of a small village. The car park is next to a field belonging to an old ramshackle farm. The hotel is immaculate with window boxes full of geraniums, not a brown leaf amongst them. The sheep field has a wonky, handmade gate; there's a rusty old bath full of brown water in the meadow.

Louise runs to the field, 'Sheepy, sheepy, do sheeps like liquorice, Mummy? Mummy, can I have a sweet for the sheep?'

'They eat grass.'

Louise pulls up grass and yells at the top of her voice, 'Sheepy, sheepy, come here. SHEEPY SHEEPYYYY! Mummy, why aren't they coming? SHEEPYYYY!'

'Our neighbours keep sheep,' Roxy says.

'Huh?' Liza says, 'who, Brent?'

'No, in Brabant.'

'Oh.'

'I used to help shear them.'

'Nice,' Jane says.

'Stupid animals.'

'They're not stupid,' Louise says.

'Those ones need shearing.'

'Do they have to be?'

'Otherwise they get maggots.'

'What?'

'Haven't they been shorn already?' Liza asks.

'They were shorn too early.'

'You can see that?' Jane asks.

'You can see it too.'

'Of course I can't,' Jane says. 'I know nothing about sheep, I'm a born and bred Amsterdammer.'

'You're not missing a thing.'

'Sounds all right to me, sheep shearing.'

'I used to help with the lambing, too.'

'Really?'

'Yes,' Roxy says. 'First they'd send me to the chemist's

to buy twenty tubes of lube.'

Liza laughs. 'No way.'

'Yeah, my Dad found it hilarious.'

It's Saturday and the restaurant is full with locals that evening. During the dessert course, a little boy comes over and stands next to their table. He's slightly bigger than Louise. He shows her his car and babbles something in French. He runs off and Louise runs after him. They go to the part of the restaurant his parents are sitting in.

'Why do your novels take place in the city?' Jane asks.

Roxy blushes. 'Have you read the other two as well?'

'Why have you gone red?'

'Have you read them?'

'You say your first book was such a piece of trash but you never blush when we talk about it.'

'I don't know.'

'What don't you know?'

'I only know that everything needs to be rewritten.'

'Everything?'

'Maybe not everything, but I'm nowhere near to knowing what does and what doesn't have to be.'

'Are you talking about your work or your marriage?' Liza asks.

'Everything,' Roxy says.

'That's too much,' Jane says. 'Why don't you write a book about your mother? You've already done your father.'

'I just wanted to get away from that place and the book allowed me to escape. But once you've finally got away, all everyone wants to hear about is where you came from.'

'I'm curious about your mother too,' Liza says, 'why she drinks and all that.'

'Maybe I'm tired of that subject.'

'You've never even written about it!'

'I lived with it for seventeen years, that seems like enough to me.'

'Seriously,' Jane begins. 'All that stuff about the sheep—people really like reading those kinds of stories. Write something about the countryside, "Back to Brabant," people love that. Something with sheep on the jacket. Always good.'

Roxy says, 'The boy next door used the get the lambs to give him blow jobs.'

'Yuck.' Jane pushes away her tarte tatin.

'You should try putting your hand in their mouths, they start sucking right away.'

'That's really disgusting, Roxy. Thanks a million, I won't be able to look at another lamb.'

'People like that don't they, though? Stuff about sheep?'

Louise throws herself unexpectedly into her arms.

'Look,' she says. She's holding a paper peacock from an ice-cream sundae.

'How nice. Were you given it?'

'No,' she says, 'pinched it.' She looks proud. The little boy on the other side of the restaurant is being carted off crying by his mother. Roxy assumes that Louise hasn't picked up on the boy's distress.

'Louise,' she says, 'that little boy's crying now, do you think that's nice?'

Louise nods angrily and says, 'Yes.'

Roxy is surprised by the answer but even more surprised by how much she is enjoying the answer. She knows she should tell her daughter off now, but she beams.

She pulls Louise onto her lap and says in a voice full of admiration, 'That isn't very kind, sweetie, is it?'

Louise happily holds up the peacock.

Jane says, 'Go and give it back, it's not yours.'

'Louise!' Liza says.

Roxy kisses her daughter. 'Too late, they've already left.'

'And stop that idiotic giggling,' Liza says.

'Come on.'

'It's not something you should be laughing about.'

'But it's funny,' Roxy says, 'I mean, interesting, the way empathy works and that ... I mean ... I thought I only had to point it out to her ... and that ...' They've left her and Roxy continues stammering about boundaries and acquired empathy, but they've seen her proud smile and there's nothing she can do to compensate.

She pulls Louise toward her. The child as a shield, the child as a weapon. She kisses her tiny head, inhales the smell of her hair, she knows she shouldn't, but just a moment of those soft cheeks, one more hit of total approval and being a single body.

'Some people are good at setting up a business,' Arthur had said, 'others are better at continuity. A person who is good for the first few years isn't necessary right for the period that comes after that.'

When she's in her room her father calls. He's on his way.

'Where are you?'

'Belgium.'

'Is there a lot of traffic?'

'I'm ploughing on.'

'Are you taking breaks?'

'I've got the radio.'

'Do I need to sing you awake?'

'Where do I need to pick you up from?'

'Louise wants to go to the seaside. They're heading toward Marseilles.'

'Flipping heck, that's a trek.'

She could say that she could meet him sooner, that she doesn't have to go to Marseilles herself, but thinking is not the same as saying it. Daddy has to come and then they'll see. Her father names a trucker's café in Marseilles. She writes down the address and shakes her head at this irrational plan. Arthur is very close now, precisely because she is sure he wouldn't understand any of this. She isn't seriously hoping that that idiot will save her, is she? Don't call my dad an idiot.

SHE WENT TO bed at the same time as Louise and fell asleep immediately, but in the middle of the night, she's wide awake again.

She remembers the sick girl in the car park and thinks about the crying boy in the restaurant. She also thinks about Marcel's wife and the baby in the football shirt but mainly about the new friends of hers who have written her off. She hates them for it. The fly is back, she wants to die but she can't because of Louise, so she hates the people who don't love her and then she hates herself again, but she can't because she needs herself for Louise and then she hates them again and carries on going in circles. She can't escape until Louise stops needing her. She feels she is approaching that moment. She moves toward it like a person with vertigo heading for the clifftop nonetheless. There has to be another way, since where will she go when she's no longer needed, and does she dare?

It is hot, she is sweating, the bed is sticky, she carefully gets up. Louise sleeps on.

Roxy stands on the doorstep to the restaurant; nobody's there. The tables are already laid for breakfast. It's four in the morning; the night is over. The morning has yet to begin. Louise was born at a moment like this, the quietest time of the night. The unfamiliar midwife in the house was so used to being the most intimate of strangers, her presence was barely noticeable. They were alone with their daughter. It would be hours before the world came to know of her existence.

She tries to remember Arthur's face that night. She pictures him sitting awkwardly on his own bed, like a visitor who has sat down on a hospital bed, wary of being in the way. She can't quite see his face.

It's a warm night. She walks across the car park in a T-shirt, shorts, and flip-flops and sits on the old fence around the sheep field. The fence is too wobbly; she jumps off, into the field.

The sheep are standing together under a shelter in the corner of the meadow. One of them has strayed from the flock and stands there chewing lethargically. When she got bored on long Sunday mornings as a child—her mother was still asleep—she'd sometimes visit her neighbour's sheep. She felt comforted by the way the sheep would move aside for her, a rare moment when the world fit around her and not the other way round. You could walk through the flock with your eyes shut. It's a pleasant memory, nothing wrong with it. It's the first time she's remembered this; she's never told anyone. She is recovering more and more of her childhood, finding bits she didn't even know she'd lost. She had to give up Arthur for them.

Ten years have been taken from her. She simply starts afresh, on the corner of Saint Vitus Street and the Molenhof, but this time he doesn't pick her up. She knows it's not possible but she doesn't know of any other way. One day she'll find Arthur again. She'll see him as she once saw him, though it sounds like a theory now, a logical thought. She can't imagine what it would be like at all.

She walks on calmly toward a sheep like a girl of ten, in a recollection that belongs to her alone, but the sheep stays where it is. She gets even closer and her bare legs touch its oily fleece.

She squats, which is difficult without high heels, and looks the sheep in its ugly, yellow eyes. It's not afraid of her; it's totally clueless.

'Go,' she says softly, but it doesn't go.

'I want you to go.'

The sheep doesn't go.

She wraps her arms around it; it lets her. Creatures like this don't survive.

'Poor silly idiot,' she says, 'I can do whatever I want to you.'

Then she hugs it even tighter, her arms under its shoulders, its dirty, oily wool against her cheek, and she overturns the animal in a single strong movement—she onto her back, the sheep onto its back. She wriggles out from underneath it. She knows a sheep can't turn over itself, certainly not this one with its thick fleece.

Soon it is panting. Its innards are pressing against its lungs, it's getting short of breath. If it lies like that for long enough it will suffocate. It's only a game, she's shown it who's boss. Now all she has to do is tip it over again.

The sheep looks even more witless on its back. It's sticking-up feet beat the air stupidly in time to its breathing. It doesn't even try to save itself.

It's hardly taken any effort, a useless enemy this one.

Typical. They're either dead, drunk, gone off, or innocent. One day she'll have to take revenge on someone. I'm sure you will. What? How pathetic, a stupid, docile sheep is about the limit of your abilities—who's the poor silly idiot here? Stop it. Pick on someone your own size. Who then? In God's name, give me someone. Don't make us laugh—you? Me, yes. You? I'll turn over the entire flock if needs be. You? Don't laugh, don't laugh for God's sake, don't laugh at me.

Roxy runs. The flock rushes away in fright but tonight Roxy will win.

Some of them cluster together; she launches herself at one of the bigger ones with a fat neck. It resists her but she has a good firm hold and there's nothing left to impress anyone with once it's on its back. Again, she throws herself at a clump of sheep and grabs whatever she can. It's better than that rodeo thing at the funfair, she clings on to whatever she gets hold of—a foot, an ear, wool.

After her third victory, she no longer looks at the results but keeps up her pace. Like a game of tag, she takes out the other children, one by one, until she has won.

Roxy looks for her flip-flops. She has to tug one out from under a sheep. Like the sheep, she's panting, but their lung capacity declines while hers only improves. She turns around briefly in the car park, surveys the battlefield and is content. There's no time to revel in her glory, she has to get back before Louise wakes up.

Her heart is pounding, her head touches her daughter's. She can't smell the child, she has brought too much with her: grass, sheep, sweat. She hears her own heart, her own breath. The beating gradually slows, her breathing becomes calmer, she fades away and smells her child, feels her, becomes her. She sniffs her hair. She kisses her neck, she kisses her cheek, the softest thing she knows. Her daughter opens her eyes and laughs. Roxy laughs. Her daughter laughs louder. She grabs her daughter and rolls backward and forward with her, like she did with the sheep.

'I want a bath,' Louise says. She loves hotel baths, only there isn't a bath here. There is noise outside: cars, voices. Roxy puts the plug into the shower tray and fills it with water, they sit in it and soap each other with the hotel soaps, keeping going until the soaps have become tiny and slip out of their fingers.

All the clothes are dirty. There's still a clean pair of jeans in her suitcase but it's too hot to be covered up. They're expensive jeans. She fetches the sewing set she put in her sponge bag and struggles to cut the legs off with the minuscule pair of scissors. The old shirt she sleeps in is perfectly all right to wear.

They enter the breakfast room bearing with them the overwhelming odour of cheap soap. Louise climbs onto her lap. Roxy feels her and barely notices which mouth she's stuffing bread into, her own mouth or her daughter's.

Jane and Liza appear at the same time as the boy from last night, along with his parents. Louise lets herself slide from her lap and runs to him. The little boy seems to have forgotten she took something from him. He shows her his cars and soon they are both sitting under the buffet table with them. Roxy feels naked without her. She doesn't know what to say to the women.

Some guests are standing at the window, pointing outside.

'What are they looking at?' Liza asks.

They leave Roxy sitting there on her own. She finds that mean. This is the way she interprets the world now—in a concise manner, understandable for three-year-olds and for people who haven't slept but fought.

'Half of the sheep seem to be dead,' Jane says.

'Half?' Roxy asks. Half. You do your best and—half.

'They can't get up again if they lie on their backs,' Liza says. 'They suffocate. They found them like that this morning.'

'Yes,' Jane says, 'I once heard something to that effect; so it's true then?'

'Terrible,' Liza says. 'What kind of person would do that?'

'A person?' Jane asks.

'Yes,' Liza says, 'it's too much of a coincidence for them all to suddenly lie down on their backs. That's not normal.'

'Bloody hell,' Jane says, 'that's really sick.'

'Yes,' Liza says.

Roxy shunts her chair back. She's feeling hot and rolls up her shirtsleeves. She looks at Louise but Louise doesn't look at her. The women stare at her arms. She is clean, she smells of soap, but she is covered in cuts and grazes.

'What happened, Roxy?' Liza asks.

'You should have seen the other one.'

'What have you done?' Jane asks.

Roxy smiles, her pride is back. No one expected this of her. She's so much more than she had expected; she is a person to be reckoned with.

'They're only sheep,' she said, 'but still.'

'No,' Liza says. 'No.'

Roxy nods and enjoys their expressions as it slowly

dawns on them. First amazement and then their pure attention.

'No,' Liza says again.

'Oh yes,' Roxy says. There's no taming her enthusiasm. She grins like a child who has performed a trick, facing a parent who is exaggerating their astonishment.

'I was so strong last night. I didn't know I had it in me.' Liza's amazement turns to disgust. Something's going wrong in that face, and then she averts her gaze.

Jane does what she's good at: she acts.

'Liza, you look after Louise. Make sure she stays inside, okay? And act normally. If anyone asks, we've gone for a smoke.'

She grabs Roxy by her arm. 'Come outside with me.'

'Louise,' Roxy says.

'Louise doesn't need you. Come.' Roxy stands up, Jane doesn't let go, she's pinching. Roxy doesn't let her see she's hurting her, of course not, she'd like that.

They enter the corridor behind the dining room that runs past the kitchen and through the back door. Jane walks quickly, almost too fast for Roxy, who is wearing her high heels. She hurries along the street, through the small village where most of the houses have roll-down shutters that are still closed.

The village stops unexpectedly at the end of the street. They come out behind a row of garages, covered in old graffiti, a sorry mix of faded brown colours. Jane finally lets go of her arm.

Roxy laughs once again; it comes out oddly. A strange giggle in the hope that Jane will join in, but Jane glares at her furiously. Finally. Now it's coming.

'Yeah, what?' Roxy says.

'WHAT?'

'Where do you want to start? You tell me. Out with it! Arthur? Louise? Marcel? My parents? Tell me! Don't hold back!'

'Huh?'

'Come on!'

'What are you talking about?'

'Come on, Jane.'

But Jane's anger seems to subside, there's only confusion left.

'Fucking hell! Say something!'

'Those sheep, Roxy.' Jane's eyes are damp.

'The sheep?'

'Yes, what else?'

'Are you blubbing about those fucking sheep?'

'Huh?'

'They've had a bloody better life than whatever you had on your plate yesterday. You didn't sit there blubbing about your rump steak!'

'Huh?'

'If you look at it in perspective ...'

'Eating meat is different from killing animals for ... for ... for ...'

'You eat them for pleasure too, don't you?'

'Christ.'

'And I put them on their backs.'

'For fun?'

'If you're worried about the way those sheep died, you should go take a look in a slaughterhouse some time.'

'I'm not worried about those bloody animals, I'm worried about you.'

It's as though the walls she's kicking have been taken away and Roxy falls flat on her face.

'About me?'

Roxy looks at the garages, at the fields in the distance, at Jane, searching for something to attack. 'About me?'

Jane remains silent. What kind of a tactic is this?

Roxy thinks about that martial arts nonsense: that you can use the other person's attack to defeat him, simply by going with it rather than fighting back.

Obviously she has to become calm now. Yes, she'll win at both calmness and self-control. 'You don't have to worry about me, even though it's very considerate of you.'

'Jesus Christ,' Jane says, 'Arthur said that you were disturbed, but I didn't know it was this bad.'

'Oh, we're going down that path, are we? Shall I tell you something about Arthur? Shall I tell you something about Arthur, then?'

'Yes, please.'

But Roxy doesn't know what she wants to tell her.

'Arthur,' Jane says, 'was a very nice, clever, opportunistic bastard, who, to my knowledge, never slaughtered a flock of sheep.'

'A flock—a flock? Come on now, how many died? Seven or so?'

'What's it to be, Roxy? Showing off or playing it down?'

Now it's pitiful all of a sudden, the sheep. That woman twists everything. Roxy's feet hurt, she sits down with her back to a dirty garage. She searches for the meaning of what she did.

In this sheltered spot, Jane says, 'If it's not that bad, those few sheep, there's no problem with me telling Louise what her mother did then, is there?'

Her daughter's name is like a punch in the gut. Roxy gasps for breath and wants to say that she's wrong, Jane can tell her daughter everything, she can twist the truth, but now Roxy suddenly understands that Jane doesn't have to twist the truth—it's bad enough as it is. She sees it through her daughter's eyes and those eyes don't lie. She desperately tries to hide behind the thought that children are loyal, she could tell her daughter there's nothing wrong with suffocating a few sheep. Give up. Give up, Roxy—she mustn't know who you are.

'Don't tell her.'

Roxy wants to throw up. She retches. It's no use. She'll have to live with everything that's inside of her.

'Don't tell Louise, please don't.'

Crying only hurts; her throat breaks. She stops and gets up with difficulty, her head bowed. Jane is wearing the Italian loafers, the ones from the funeral. Roxy doesn't want to be seen but the only thing she can do is make sure she doesn't see anyone else looking at her. She totters and feels Jane's hand on her arm.

Jane rolls down Roxy's shirtsleeves. 'We'll put those like that.' She does up the cuffs. She wipes Roxy's hair from her face and pats the dirt off her shorts. She tries to limit the damage. The woman is good—Arthur often said so—always professional, an assistant worth gold. Roxy knows Jane won't leave her until the time is right.

'Your mascara has run.'

Roxy turns away from her, wets her fingers with spit and rubs under her eyes.

'Come on.'

They walk back along the ugly street; blinds start to open.

'Look up and smile,' Jane says, 'and when we get back inside, you're to go directly to your room and pack your case. We'll check out and I'll come and fetch you when we leave. We'll take care of Louise.'

They hold their heads high and walk smiling along the street, two tourists who are up and about early.

'We're going to the seaside,' Jane says.

'Yes, the seaside,' Roxy says. A wooden dialogue between two poor actors.

Roxy packs her case and shivers like a wet child. When she's finished, she doesn't sit down but stands and waits. There's noise outside, Roxy stands at a distance from the window. She jumps when there's a knock on the door.

'It's me, Jane.'

Jane says, 'Put your sunglasses on.'

Roxy gets the handbag her glasses are in, she tries to obey Jane as quickly as possible, to limit the nuisance she is, to limit her presence, herself, but her handbag falls and the contents tumble out. Jane kneels.

'No,' Roxy says, 'I'll do it.' With her shaking hands, she can hardly get anything back in her bag. Jane tidies everything up, hands Roxy her sunglasses and zips the handbag shut.

'Thank you.'

She follows Jane out of the hotel and into the car park.

There is a pile covered with orange plastic in the field. A few sheep are grazing and one sheep is walking oddly through the field, lurching. A large man is attentively following the sheep at a short distance, taking care that the sheep doesn't hurt itself, that it doesn't bump into anything. The man holds his arms spread slightly, his big hands open, ready to catch the animal but also to bless it.

'Come on.' Jane has opened the car door for her, the passenger seat. Roxy gets in and turns around immediately. Liza is sitting next to Louise, reading a book to her.

'Hi darling,' Roxy says.

'Shhh,' Louise says.

'... and the wolf bends down, looks through the keyhole and sees something that makes his mouth water: three ... pink ... piglets.'

They drive, the seatbelt alarm goes off. Roxy puts her seatbelt on.

The sky is clear. It's already hot but not yet busy on the roads. Jane drives slowly in the right-hand lane, icily calm. Roxy keeps her sunglasses on and feels a wave of nostalgia about the funeral. She'd like nothing more than to return to that moment. It's the only thing she wants: to go back to being pitiful, a loser. Or to sit next to her father in the truck again; she should never have felt ashamed of him. She promises herself never to feel ashamed again. She's tired and wants to sleep, she can't sleep now—she has to sing: day-o, day-ay-ay-o.

They only stop to buy food, to fill up the tank, or to pee. They eat in the car as they press on. Liza focuses all of her energy on the child—stories, jokes, songs, again and again, she puts her heart and soul into it. Roxy doesn't exist for Louise. Jane only opens her mouth about practical matters.

'Can you open this bottle for me?'

Roxy does it soundlessly and makes sure her fingers don't touch Jane's when she's handing her the bottle, or a sandwich, or a serviette. She travels with these people like an Untouchable, continually trying to catch a glimpse in the rear mirror of the child with Arthur's eyes.

In the afternoon, when they stop at a petrol station, she wants to lift her daughter up, but before she's got to her, Liza and Louise have run to the toilets, hand in hand.

She once thought about slowly transferring her into someone else's hands. How can it be this easy for her child not to need her? Opportunistic creature. Good for you, you know what you need, you're my daughter, you're strong.

Jane refuels the car.

'I'll go to the till,' Roxy says.

Jane doesn't even nod.

Roxy pays with the card from her and Arthur's joint account and withdraws a large sum of money from the machine near the counter. She comes outside very slowly, her gaze focused on her feet, giving the others the chance to drive off without her. She looks up and the car has indeed gone from the pump.

'Don't panic,' she says. 'You've got no reason to panic.'

She walks around the side of the petrol station. The suv is in one of the parking spaces. They're still there. Relief. More time. Liza is swinging Louise around in circles, Jane is smoking a cigarette, leaning against the bonnet. A family she'd like to belong to.

She calls her father.

'Just putting you on the hands-free.'

'Do you use a hands-free?'

'Can't call in the cab, much too dangerous.'

Her father, a responsible man. Even her father is a responsible man. Everything has to be rewritten, it's true; she'll listen to her father.

'End of the afternoon, I'll be there by then.'

Louise is picking flowers in the verge; Liza and Jane are discussing something.

Roxy fixes a time to meet her father at the truck stop café. Jane and Liza hug. Roxy hangs up. She waits until the women have separated and goes over to them.

Louise holds up her hand. 'I picked flowers for you.'

Roxy squats. 'Gorgeous.' She accepts the dandelions.

'Do you want some more?' Louise is already making her way to the tiny, dirty flowerbed next to the lay-by.

'My father is in the area,' Roxy says. 'He can pick me up this evening.'

'What are you talking about?' Jane asks.

'He can pick us up. You can carry on with the car. I've taken out some money for the journey back. I've only got one bank card. I think you can get quite far with it.' She holds out the wad of cash. No one takes it.

'Put the money away,' Liza says.

'It's no problem,' Roxy says.

'Put the money away.'

'Seriously.'

'I want you to put the money away.'

Roxy puts the stack of notes in the back pocket of her jeans. 'But you can simply carry on in the car.'

'*Simply*?' Liza says.

'Yes.'

'Fucking hell,' Liza says. 'Simply! We were *simply* going to the seaside, weren't we? We'll start by going to a hotel tonight and have a bite to eat and a glass of wine, or two, it'll all be really simple and, who knows, we might even get bored, and you'll act normal, you won't tip any sheep onto their backs and you won't lie on your back yourself—all very simple—and tomorrow we'll simply go to the seaside and maybe the next day we'll simply go again.'

Louise has joined them, a bunch of wilting weeds in her hand. 'Are we going to the seaside?'

'Tomorrow,' Roxy says.

'And now get in the car,' Liza says.

In the car Louise starts singing, 'Are we nearly there yet? Are we nearly there yet?'

Roxy is sitting awkwardly on the wad of banknotes and tries to get them out of her trouser pocket and into her handbag without anybody noticing. The money falls and she goes to bend down but does so too quickly, locking the seatbelt; she tries it again but again the seatbelt locks. She moves back again and very calmly leans forward so that the seatbelt gives.

'What are you up to?' Jane asks.

'Nothing,' Roxy says.

'With that money?'

'I'm putting it away.'

'Is your dad really in the area?'

'Yes.'

'For his work?'

'Kind of.'

'Kind of?'

'For me.'

'Why?'

'If I ... If we ... If you don't ... or I don't ...'

The words are like the seatbelt, they begin to flow smoothly but soon get stuck.

Roxy has another go, 'I thought that you ... I didn't want ...'

Nobody wants to know what the next words are and she gives up. Giving up is lovely, a sweet, lazy pain she welcomes with a sigh. It's not a decision—that would be crazy—no one can make a decision like that; it's a form of surrender.

When they arrive at the hotel, she doesn't have to try hard for her hands to shake, to drop bags, move slowly. Her helplessness is just under the surface; you just have to stop trying. The others automatically start looking after the child and she goes with them to Liza's room. It's not a decision, it's not a deed. It's finally letting things run their natural course.

She packs a small bag in her room, like a person only going away for a short time. She waits five minutes and then cautiously opens her hotel room door, no one in the corridor. She closes the door without making a sound.

Her flight began earlier, she recognizes it from previous experiences, the way you slowly dissolve in your own existence, the way her parents became strangers and all she had to do was let herself float away, until the familiar territory was out of reach.

She leaves an envelope containing the money and the car keys at the reception and asks them to call her a taxi. She waits outside.

The trucker's café is nearby. It's next to the motorway. In the back of the taxi, she feels the pain increasing with every kilometre she puts between herself and her child, but some people deserve pain. 'I'll fetch her again later,' she mutters to herself. It's the only way to be able to drive away.

She steps through a plastic fly-curtain, the café is full. There's a large bar with people eating at it. She calmly looks around, in search of her father. He always knows how to find a good place where he won't stand out and can instantly make friends. The shaking has stopped and the calmness of a person who has escaped comes over her.

That time she got into the Golden Nissan on the street corner, she didn't experience a moment's doubt. She had surrendered herself to Arthur and he accepted it, completely. There were people who found it strange; she couldn't be doing with them. Through his existence, through their togetherness, she could observe the world without doubt. If you've ever felt that, seen it, a world without doubt, it's not easy to give it up.

The truckers' restaurant smells of roast chicken and familiar greasy fumes hang in the air. She is still wearing sunglasses to hide her red eyes, still wearing those crookedly cut-off jeans and the heels. The men look at her. She's barely slept, she knows she looks awful but the aloofness of someone who no longer cares makes her attractive.

He is sitting at the bar, deep in conversation with a couple of other Dutch men. She walks up to him.

'Beauty!' he cries. 'Where's the little 'un?'

'She's coming later,' Roxy says, the men next to him listening in.

'Come,' he says and is already standing up, looking for a table for two.

The skinny old man he's sitting next to asks Roxy, 'Can I buy you a drink?'

She says, 'Another time, okay?' The men next to him laugh. Roxy had forgotten how good she was at this, the ease with which she joins in in places like this, an ease she never knew with Arthur's friends. She feels a strange mixture of disappointment and relief; this is where she belongs.

'I've ordered spare ribs,' her father says. 'What do you want?' A waitress brings them beer.

'I'll just have the same.'

Her father holds up two fingers to the waitress, pointing at the beer and the menu.

'Spare ribs,' he says, without being embarrassed at his clumsiness.

Roxy sinks down and takes off her glasses.

'Good morning to you,' her father says.

'Yeah.'

'What is it then? Have you lot fallen out?'

'Things went ... a bit wrong.'

'That lezza. She is one, I knew it.'

'It's not their fault.'

'You've always been much too good to other people.'

'No, I ... yesterday, I ...' she looks out of the window. 'We were staying at a hotel in a village last night. There were sheep next door.'

'Stupid animals.'

The waitress sets down a glass of beer in front of her. Roxy drinks.

'... I turned ... I turned them onto their backs, in the night because ...' She shrugs. 'I turned them onto their backs.'

'As long as you put them back on their feet again afterward.' He roars with laughter. Roxy peers into her glass and doesn't laugh.

'Oh,' he says, 'you left them like that?'

She nods.

'No, they can't take that, no.'

'No.'

'What now, then? Do you have to reimburse them for the lot?'

She looks at him. 'We ran away.'

'They don't know who done it?'

'No.'

'Oooh,' he says. He takes a big sip of beer and wipes his mouth with the back of his hand.

Roxy looks for the shock in his face, his disapproval, but can't find it. He looks happy. His look is directed at her. She can't take her eyes off the man who is happy to see her. Maybe this is love. She smiles.

Her father says, 'I once rode a Shetland pony with my fat gut when I was drunk. We all do things like that sometimes.'

Her smile freezes. 'A pony?'

'Yeah, one of them little 'uns.'

Her eyes drop down to his body. 'And then?'

'What?'

She tries to keep on smiling, she owes him one now. Smile. He has driven to Marseilles for her.

'And the pony?'

'Tut, tut, Missy. No, you're an animal lover.'

The spare ribs arrive. They're always quick in truckers' places, you don't want moody drivers. Her father tucks in eagerly. The nausea she felt this morning has returned in full glory. Roxy adds a little pony with a broken back to her own doings. She picks up her knife and frees the flesh between the ribs. She ignores her nausea and chews the ribs. Keep going, act, move, eat; there is sweat on her brow.

'Everybody makes stupid mistakes,' her father says. 'Everyone, and that's exactly what you two always forgot.'

'You two?'

'Arthur and you. No one's better than anyone else.'

Roxy drinks her beer faster than her father.

'Just like the good old days,' he says.

'Just like the good old days.' She knows she can't leave with him. This escape route has been cut off. She can't go with him and she won't be able to explain it to him. She'll disappoint him, but not now. There has to be a better moment.

'When's the little 'un coming then?'

'She's not coming.'

'What do you mean?'

'Car sick. She gets car sick all the time. She's better off going with Jane and Liza for a bit … beach holiday. Better.' It no longer matters what she says, the atmosphere has to stay nice. This can't go on for much longer, and after that it'll be done; he'll end up cursing her.

'She's mad about Liza.'

'She's a lovely lass.'

'It's just the two of us,' she says in English.

'Speak the language God gave you.'

'Sorry.'

He suggests driving to Poland, like they'd done back then.

'Why not?' Roxy uses the serviette to wipe her forehead.

'Otherwise you could just drop her off at your ma's.' He's not joking.

Roxy drops her knife and fork and pushes her plate away.

'Don't you like it?' He gestures at her food.

'She's not going to Mum's.'

Her father lays down his cutlery too.

'She'd only be alone otherwise.'

'Have you gone barking mad?'

'You know, Roxy, the problem with Arthur?'

'Don't do it.'

'Do you know what the problem was?'

'Don't do it, Dad.'

'Don't do what?'

'Arthur was my husband.'

'I've driven all the way to France for you, Missy.'

'And I appreciate it too.'

'The lady appreciates it.'

Roxy dips her fingers into the bowl of water. 'Shit.' There's lemon in it and it burns into the cuts on her hands.

'What?'

'Lemon.' She looks for her serviette, it has fallen onto the floor. She bends down.

'Nothing wrong with your ma.'

She comes back up again immediately.

'Jesus Christ, Dad.'

'No, you're the mother of the year.'

'Excuse me?'

'But it doesn't matter, doll.' He smiles.

Roxy tries to smile back but doesn't manage.

'You're just like me,' her father says. 'We're free agents. We're the same.'

Roxy gets up.

'What?'

'I don't feel well.'

She walks out of the café.

Outside, she stands between the trucks. How often can a person be wrong?

'Roxy?'

He's followed her. That's not like her father. He needs her. 'Are you ill?'

'No.'

Her feet hurt. She takes off her heels and now she's shorter than he. The tarmac is much too hot for bare feet and yet she stays standing there.

'I can't come with you, Dad.'

'What's this now?'

'I'm not coming.'

'What am I doing here, then?'
'Sorry.'
'Yes.'
'Yes.'
'And now?'
'I have to go back.'
'Home?'
'To Louise.'

On the Design

As book design is an integral part of the reading experience, we would like to acknowledge the work of those who shaped the form in which the story is housed.

Tessa van der Waals (Netherlands) is responsible for the cover design, cover typography, and art direction of all World Editions books. She works in the internationally renowned tradition of Dutch Design. Her bright and powerful visual aesthetic maintains a harmony between image and typography and captures the unique atmosphere of each book. She works closely with internationally celebrated photographers, artists, and letter designers. Her work has frequently been awarded prizes for Best Dutch Book Design.

This cover photo was taken in Brooklyn by Patrice Hauser. Hauser was a fighter pilot in the French Navy, but left the army to pursue his passion for photography and travel. He currently works as a magazine editor, journalist, and photographer. Our Art Director, Tessa van der Waals, looked at billboards and drive-in restaurant signs for inspiration for the type: 'A title like Roxy begs for a monumental presence on the cover.'

The cover has been edited by lithographer Bert van der Horst of BFC Graphics (Netherlands).

Suzan Beijer (Netherlands) is responsible for the typography and careful interior book design of all World Editions titles.

The text on the inside covers and the press quotes are set in Circular, designed by Laurenz Brunner (Switzerland) and published by Swiss type foundry Lineto.

All World Editions books are set in the typeface Dolly, specifically designed for book typography. Dolly creates a warm page image perfect for an enjoyable reading experience. This typeface is designed by Underware, a European collective formed by Bas Jacobs (Netherlands), Akiem Helmling (Germany), and Sami Kortemäki (Finland). Underware are also the creators of the World Editions logo, which meets the design requirement that 'a strong shape can always be drawn with a toe in the sand.'